SOME EIGHTEEN SUMMERS

After eighteen years living a sheltered life as a vicar's daughter in Norfolk, Debbie Meredith takes work as a companion to the wealthy Mrs. Caroline Dewbrey in Yorkshire. Travelling by train, she meets the handsome and charming Hugh Stacey. However, before long, Debbie is wondering why Mrs. Dewbrey lavishes so much attention on her. And what of her son Alec's stance against her involvement with Hugh? Debbie then finds that she's just a pawn embroiled in a tragic vendetta . . .

Books by Lillie Holland
in the Linford Romance Library:

LOVE'S ALIEN SHORE
THE ECHOING BELLS
AFTER THE HARVEST
NOT AS A COWARD

LILLIE HOLLAND

SOME EIGHTEEN SUMMERS

Complete and Unabridged

LINFORD
Leicester

First published in Great Britain in 1972

First Linford Edition
published 2013

British Library CIP Data

Holland, Lillie.
Some eighteeen summers.- -
(Linford romance library)
1. Love stories.
2. Large type books.
I. Title II. Series
823.9'2-dc23

ISBN 978-1-4448-1396-8

Published by
F. A. Thorpe (Publishing)
Anstey, Leicestershire

Set by Words & Graphics Ltd.
Anstey, Leicestershire
Printed and bound in Great Britain by
T. J. International Ltd., Padstow, Cornwall

This book is printed on acid-free paper

To the memory of my parents

1

I shall never forget the day following my eighteenth birthday. It was the day that I left home and went as a companion to Mrs. Caroline Dewbrey of Ditchford Hall, near Halifield in Yorkshire.

It was like a dream saying goodbye to my father and mother and sister Emma. It had all been so sudden — I had not even known of Mrs. Dewbrey's existence until six weeks before.

'Goodbye, Debbie,' said Papa, embracing me in the carriage. 'Remember what I told you.' Mama embraced me without speaking, her face pale and drawn.

'Goodbye, my darling,' she whispered.

'Goodbye, Mama.' I held her close to me. Emma clung to me, looking wide-eyed and scared under her sailor hat. I had a swift, poignant thought of her clumsy little fingers brushing my hair, and helping me dress in the mornings. I would miss her dreadfully, and she would me. My family stepped out of the railway carriage as the guard was preparing to whistle the train off.

'I'll write as soon as I get there,' I said, swallowing hard. 'Goodbye, goodbye . . . '

Then I sat back in my corner seat, feeling lonely, frightened, and excited all at once. Apart from myself, the carriage was empty. Papa had put my baggage on the rack. I glanced at the matching valises and the hat-box.

My parents' gift for my eighteenth birthday.

'You will need nice valises for travelling,' Papa had said. I hadn't known how soon I would be travelling, though. Now, of course, I realised the gifts were very practical.

That morning six weeks ago!

I sat thinking about it, while the Norfolk landscape slipped by.

* * *

It had begun like any other, except that I had woken a bit earlier than usual. High in the sycamore tree outside my window, a thrush was singing loudly. I craned my neck to see him, and my long black braid of hair swung heavily when I moved.

It was spring, but my life would go on as usual. I would help Mama in her duties, teach at Sunday School, sketch and embroider. Plenty of girls were married at my age. I supposed some day I might marry, too. But whom? The only men I ever seemed to meet were dull, earnest young curates, and, indeed, what more could I hope for, as the daughter of a poor, country clergyman?

'Life consists of doing one's duty,' Papa would say. But outside the vicarage, the first wild flowers were pushing up in the hedgerows, and the lambs were frollicking in the green meadows . . .

I heard Bessie's gentle tap at the door.

'Good day, Miss Debbie.' She stood there with the hot water, a smile on her pleasant face.

'Good day. Thank you, Bessie.'

I took the water from her and poured it out myself, as I knew that Bessie had many duties, and could not act as full time lady's maid.

Emma and I helped each other dress in the mornings. When I had washed I slipped into a cotton wrapper, and went to her little room. She was washing herself; a very thin twelve-year-old, clad in her chemise, her arms like sticks.

She smiled at me a trifle dolefully, as though she was still not properly awake. We weren't a scrap alike to look at. She was fair and pale, rather like Mama must have been in her younger days. I had black hair and up-tilted blue-green eyes, and when I smiled I dimpled, which made me look rather too young for my liking. My cheeks were too round, also, and, I feared, too pink.

'Let me do your hair, Emma,' I said.

Afterwards she helped me dress,

lacing me too tightly as usual, although I would never admit it.

There was something strange in Mama's manner that morning, though she greeted me affectionately as always. I wondered if she had a headache.

'Tell Papa breakfast is ready,' she said.

I knocked on the door of his study, and heard his usual muttered, 'Come in.'

The study was an untidy yet comfortable looking room, with book-lined walls, and Papa's desk piled up with papers, letters and old sermons. His spectacles were just a little bit crooked on his nose, and I straightened them gently.

'Breakfast is ready, Papa.'

'Oh, yes. Yes, my dear.'

He looked at me without smiling, and I felt there was something worrying both my parents.

I went back into the dining room with Papa following, and we had family prayers as usual.

I noticed Mama hardly ate any breakfast. I asked her if she had a headache.

'Just a slight one, Debbie,' she said, passing her hand over her forehead. I could remember her hair being much fairer when I was a child; the same shade as Emma's in fact. It had darkened to a mid-brown, and for the first time I noticed streaks of grey at her temples.

'Mama, you look tired,' I exclaimed. 'Can't you rest in your room this morning? I'll see Cook, and attend to everything else.'

After a half-hearted protest, she agreed to lie down for a while. We could not afford a governess for Emma and myself, but Papa had taken on the task of my education and that of my two brothers up to a certain age. He had taught me well, and I was now able to teach Emma. However, she was not sorry when I told her there would be no lessons that day, as I would be too busy.

When Mama had gone to her room, I

went into the kitchen to see Mrs. Henessy, our cook.

'Good day, Miss Debbie,' she said, her round face creasing into a smile. She and Bessie comprised our domestic staff.

'Good day. I've come to discuss luncheon,' I said. 'Mama has a headache, and is lying down.'

Afterwards I went up to my mother's room, as I had done so often in my childhood. She was lying fully clothed on the big fourposter bed, one hand over her forehead.

'Do you need anything, Mama?' I asked.

'No dear, I shall rise for luncheon.'

I sat on the chair beside her bed, tracing with my fingers the raised pattern on the snowy counterpane. A gust of rain spattered against the window.

'Debbie, how would you feel about going away?' asked Mama suddenly.

'Going away?' I repeated. The idea took my breath away for a moment. 'To go — where?' I asked hesitantly.

My mother raised herself on her elbow.

'Has the idea of getting a post ever appealed to you?' she enquired.

'A post?' I was incredulous. 'As what — surely not a *governess?* Am I such an encumbrance?'

'I never said as a governess,' put in Mama quickly. 'Something rather special is being offered to you. Believe me, my darling, I need you here. It is for your sake that I am prepared to let you go. Papa and I have talked this over. It will be an opportunity to have things and do things which you cannot do under our roof.'

'Please tell me what you mean, Mama,' I said, a trifle impatiently. 'I am well content to stay here.'

That was not strictly true, though. I was not well content; for a long time now a great restlessness had been stirring within me. It was this restlessness which made me feel the strange pangs of envy when I saw the cottage maidens out in their Sunday finery.

'A lady in Yorkshire would like you to be her companion,' said my mother, watching me closely.

'A lady in Yorkshire? But I have no acquaintance with a lady in Yorkshire,' I said, puzzled. At the same time, excitement rose in me.

'Until just after your birth we lived in Yorkshire,' Mama reminded me. 'This lady was known to us, very slightly, many years ago. She knows we have a daughter, and she thinks it would be a good idea if you were to stay with her for a while.'

'Why — but this lady must be old!' I exclaimed. 'I could not be a companion to an elderly lady — I would be bored!'

The expression on Mama's face silenced me. I realised with a little shock of surprise that the whole thing had already been arranged.

'No doubt she will see that you have some young companionship,' said Mama. 'Why should you be bored? And you should make the best of companions — you read aloud very nicely, you sketch and paint, and you play the piano and sing very charmingly. You have the accomplishments expected of a gentlewoman.'

'But who is this lady? If she needs companionship, why has she picked on me? Is she rich?'

Was it my imagination, or was there bitterness in Mama's usually carefully controlled voice when she replied?

'Rich? Yes, Debbie, she is very rich. She is Mrs. Caroline Dewbrey, and she lives in Ditchford Hall, a large, beautiful place in its own grounds.'

'If she has wealth,' I persisted, 'why should she want one particular girl to be her companion? Surely she has relations?' My mother said nothing.

'How did you get to know her?' I continued. 'Through Papa's duties, I suppose?'

'Yes.'

My mother didn't seem disposed to discuss this point very fully.

'I am sure you will be happy there,'

she said hopefully. Although this was a total surprise to me, now I thought about it, there had been worried looks and murmured conversations between my parents for several weeks.

I was the cause of the shadow which had hung over our tranquil house. I wanted to know more about this new life which awaited me, and why I was being despatched like this. Mama had stopped talking; the colour had drained from her face again.

An unbearable pang shot through me at the idea of leaving her, for whatever she said, the unhappiness in her eyes told me that she did not wish me to go. And if she did not wish it, why was I having to?

'What does Papa think about it?' I asked wonderingly.

'He thinks you should take this opportunity.'

Life consists of doing one's duty, I thought, mentally echoing the words which I had heard so often on Papa's lips. Clearly, then, my parents thought it was my duty to take up this post, and their duty to let me go. But why? That was something which Mama was being very reticent about.

I smiled, looking at her anxious face. I would try to play my part.

'When will I have to go?' I asked.

'In a few weeks — we would like you to have your eighteenth birthday at home.' She looked relieved. 'You must have one or two new dresses and bonnets. We will make a list of the things you need. Once you take up your post, I have no doubt Mrs. Dewbrey will pay you generously for your services.'

This was interesting. From Papa I received a modest allowance which ensured that I was always neatly, if plainly dressed. I also spent some of the money on books, and on the pretty fripperies so dear to the hearts of all girls.

But now I was to be paid, and paid generously. Surprise, excitement, curiosity, all rose inside me. I wanted to rush and tell my best friend Georgina

Riddle all about it.

Mama seemed as though she had read my thoughts.

'For the time being, don't say too much outside the home,' she warned.

'But, Mama, what am I to tell them? Georgina, and the Hilton sisters? I can't just go away — disappear into thin air.' Mama seemed unsure what to say.

'I shall have to tell Georgina something,' I pointed out.

'Yes . . . but let me talk things over with your Papa first. Now just let me rest until luncheon, Debbie.'

I withdrew, and went into my own room. Opening my wardrobe door, I examined the contents. I had only one silk gown, a blue one. I lifted it out, and examined it critically. Not quite as modish as I would have liked. Two plain day dresses, and one of muslin. I sighed, and closed the door again.

I looked round the familiar room, at my bed with its many-coloured crocheted coverlet, and the cupboard full of treasured books and toys, kept from my childhood.

Fear and shyness suddenly overwhelmed me. I should be frightened and lonely in a strange grand house, with a strange, grand old lady to please.

Who would help me to dress in the mornings? Would I have to manage with no help at all? I would miss Emma so much.

My brothers, John and Albert, were at boarding school, but I used to look forward to their holidays. I was great friends with both of them. The family life which was so dear to me would cease. Usually I wrote in my diary last thing at night, but that day I was unable to wait.

I took my diary out of my bureau, and recorded the fact that I was going as a companion to a Mrs. Caroline Dewbrey, in the county of Yorkshire.

2

The next few weeks were busy ones. My parents agreed that it was all right to tell Georgina about things. She was surprised and upset at first, but also, I fancied, a trifle envious.

However, she offered me a vast quantity of narrow white lace which she and her mother had crocheted and tatted during the winter evenings.

'You may as well have some to trim your new petticoats with,' she said, rather sadly. 'And I'll let you have the pattern of my green dress to take to the dressmaker. You always liked it.'

Emma had been told that I was going away, and although she had said little, I felt the child was puzzled by it.

I asked Mama if it would be necessary for me to write to Mrs. Dewbrey concerning my appointment, but she replied that Papa had dealt with the matter. I turned my attention to refurbishing my wardrobe. As I had expected, Mama looked with a critical eye at the pattern I had borrowed from Georgina.

'Isn't it — well, rather pretentious?' she enquired slowly. 'I mean, is it in the best of taste?'

'I like it,' I replied obstinately. 'Besides, it would offend Georgina if I didn't have it made up in this style.'

'I suppose so,' said Mama sighing.

'Anyway,' I said, in a burst of rebellion, 'I'm practically eighteen, and I should have a say in what I'm going to wear. And I want a dress in a sort of blue-green, the colour of my eyes.'

Mama looked shocked and disapproving as she always did if I talked like that.

I longed to cry out that there was nothing sinful in wanting beautiful clothes; in wanting to look beautiful.

But that meant you wished to be admired, and that again was wrong. It seemed to me, that kind and gentle though they were, my parents lacked all understanding of a young girl's desires and needs. And yet, surely Mama had been young herself once?

Surprisingly, she gave in over the matter of the new dress, and the day when I was to take up my new post in Yorkshire grew steadily nearer.

One morning, I asked Papa outright how he had got to know Mrs. Dewbrey. He paused before replying.

'Before I got a living here, I was curate in the village of Swalewell outside Halifield.'

'Did you know her very well?'

'No, not very well, my dear.'

'She must have thought highly of you,' I said slowly. 'To remember you all these years — and to want a daughter of yours as a companion.'

A look of pain passed over my father's face, and I thought it wiser to drop the subject. I tried again, though, another day.

'Of course,' I said, half to myself, and half to Papa, 'if I'm not happy there, I don't have to stay.'

'I ask you, Debbie, to give it a twelvemonth.'

'A twelvemonth, Papa! Why, Mama never said so!'

'It would scarcely cross her mind that you would not be able to endure life in such pleasant surroundings.'

'Material things do not matter — so you and Mama have told me many times.'

'In many ways they do not,' said Papa somewhat dubiously. 'We must always endeavour to be content in that state of life into which it has pleased God to call us.'

'That state of life . . . ' I repeated softly.

'Life is full of surprises,' went on my father more briskly. 'We never know what lies ahead, Debbie.'

I wondered if he was cheering me up, or preparing me for the future. Up till then life had held few surprises for me, apart from the occasional unexpected treat. As for my parents, their days passed in a monotonous round of duty.

Indeed, the only surprise I could think of was that Mrs. Dewbrey had wanted me in her home.

I was to travel to Halifield the day after my eighteenth birthday. From my parents I had a gift of handsome travelling bags, and Emma had made me a pin-cushion, and a bag for hair-combings with her own hands.

John and Albert had sent me an obscure novel entitled *The Making of Margaret*. Cook and Bessie had bought me a pair of slippers between them, and Georgina had given me a charming brooch. Most of the day was taken up with feverish preparations for the morrow, so that my eighteenth birthday was not the joyous event I had looked forward to.

I went to bed that night with my head aching, and lay awake for a long time. When I did go to sleep it seemed only five minutes before Bessie was at the door with hot water. Emma and Mama came with me and Papa in the dog-cart. It was a sharp, cool sort of day.

I looked round at the flat country landscape, and wondered when next I would see it. None of us spoke on the journey; Mama was pale but composed, and Emma unwontedly quiet sitting next to her. At the station a porter hurried forward to help with the baggage, and a few minutes later I was sitting alone in the carriage. It was all over; the kisses, the goodbyes, the hands waving until there was no one to wave to . . .

★ ★ ★

I jerked myself back into the present, all too aware of the lump in my throat. I picked up the novel which my brothers had sent me, and tried to read it. But the print was blurred, and I had to dab my eyes. After a while I became more self-possessed, and spent my time between reading and looking through the window.

The train continued steadily northwards; we were out of Norfolk, and in

Lincolnshire. We stopped at Spalding, but there were very few people about, and I still had the carriage to myself. Papa had impressed upon me that I would be changing at Doncaster, but that would not be for some time yet. I had eaten nothing at breakfast, and now I felt my appetite returning. Cook had packed some patties and a few dainties, which I unpacked and ate. Afterwards I must have drifted off to sleep, because the next thing I knew a raucous voice was shouting:

'Doncaster! Doncaster!'

I jumped up in a flurry, let down the window, and hailed a passing porter. I felt quite flustered, but he came to my assistance, and before long I was safely installed in a first class compartment of another train.

Again I was alone, although that was not really surprising, as it was a weekday, and not many people seemed to be travelling to Halifield.

The train was whistled off, and again I sat and watched the landscape slip by.

Some time later the train drew up at a small, country station, and I saw two gentlemen on the platform.

They each had a light valise, and walked along towards the first class compartments.

The younger and fairer man saw me sitting there; our eyes met, and the next moment he opened the door.

'Excuse me, madam, are these seats occupied?'

He removed his hat as he spoke, bowing slightly.

'They are not, sir,' I replied, feeling myself blush. He and his companion entered the carriage, and put their valises on the luggage rack. The fair young man was beautifully dressed in a suit of exquisite cut and excellent cloth. My eyes were modestly dropped, and I could see his boots were of the softest, most expensive leather. I sat demurely, with my novel in my hand.

How handsome the young man was!

He had fair, wavy hair, and a narrow, aristocratic looking face. He was tall and slender and elegant, above all dreams of masculine elegance. In fact, he was like the sort of men Georgina and I had dreamed about; the sort which girls in novels seemed to meet.

His travelling companion was different. He was a good deal older; in his thirties, I guessed.

He was dark and fresh-faced, neatly, but not elegantly dressed. Nevertheless, he had the bearing of a gentleman.

'Excuse me,' said the fair one, when they were settled in the carriage — 'Do you mind if we smoke? If you find it annoys you . . . '

'Not at all, sir,' I replied. 'Pray smoke if you wish.'

'Thank you.'

He smiled at me and lit a cigar, but the other gentleman seemed disinclined to smoke. He opened a newspaper, and appeared to give it his full attention.

'Travelling by train can be tedious,' said the fair one. 'Particularly if it's a long journey. Of course you can't have been travelling long, ma'am. You look as fresh as if you had just stepped on the train.'

Wonder of wonders — he was actually paying me compliments!

'I started my journey at Norwich, sir,' I said.

'And you are still travelling.'

I knew that Mama would not have approved of this conversation, but what else could I do but answer the young man's questions civilly?

Papa had said I was to be sure not to get into a carriage with a man in, but he never said what I should do if any men got into mine.

'I'm going to Halifield,' he said, lounging back, the cigar held with casual grace in his well-shaped hand.

'I'm going there too,' I said.

'I've been attending a house party.'

'Indeed?' I said, smiling. 'I hope you found it enjoyable.'

'Enjoyable enough, if one likes that sort of thing.'

'And do you?'

'It depends. If the company there is

agreeable, I do. Are you fond of house parties?'

The question took me by surprise, but I was not going to admit to this strange young man that I had never been to a house party in my life. I replied airily that I did not mind them. I thought that was a good answer, as it did not commit me.

I had taken my bonnet off some time before, but I was glad it was a new, smart one, as was my dove-grey travelling cape and dress.

I *must* look elegant, I thought; nice enough to make this young gentleman admire me, anyway.

'I take it you belong to Norwich, then,' he went on.

'I come from a little village a few miles out of it,' I said.

I was certainly not going to tell him all my business, least of all was I going to tell him that I was taking up a position as a companion. I could see that he was a gentleman of some means, and as I did not expect to meet him once our train journey was over, I saw no reason to part with any details of my private affairs. What he chose to tell me was up to him.

Mama had always impressed upon me that it was vulgar to ask people questions, yet I knew that this young man sitting opposite me would never do anything vulgar. I came to the conclusion that he was asking these questions because he was interested in me.

'I live close to a village outside Halifield,' he said. 'When the London season is over, I confess I am very glad to return.'

I smiled without speaking.

'Are you fond of reading novels?' was his next question, glancing at the book on the seat beside me.

'Too fond,' I replied with a laugh. 'I am afraid I am often reading when I should be doing something else.'

'I read a lot, too. I should really introduce myself. My name is Hugh Stacey — and you are Miss . . . ?'

'Deborah Meredith,' I said, after a

slight hesitation.

'Miss Meredith, let me introduce to you my companion — Mr. James Dryden.'

The other gentleman put down his newspaper and bowed in my direction. He smiled at both of us in an indulgent sort of way; it was plain that he himself did not wish to join in the conversation. There was nothing rude in his attitude; he merely wished to read his newspaper in peace.

'I don't think I know any Merediths,' said Mr. Stacey. 'Still, knowing you is enough.'

I thought this was very saucy of him, and looked through the window at the somewhat nondescript countryside we were passing through.

'Are you fond of Dickens' novels?' was the next question.

'I love them.'

We began to discuss books, and we were surprised and pleased to find that we shared the same tastes in literature.

The porter at Doncaster had told me

that I would have to change trains again at a station outside Leeds. I asked Mr. Stacey about it just to make sure.

'Don't worry, Miss Meredith. It's a few miles ahead — and we'll take care of you. We're going to Halifield too, so you can hardly go wrong, can you?'

'Oh, I'm not worried,' I said. 'It's merely that I'm not familiar with this part of the country.'

I wished to appear the experienced traveller which I most certainly was not. At this point Mr. Dryden lowered his newspaper slightly, and glanced across at me. He had keen, light grey eyes, and I found his gaze disconcerting. I felt he knew, as surely as if I had told him, that this was the first time I had travelled such a distance alone.

I wondered what Georgina would think could she see me now with two gentlemen in attendance; Mr. Stacey so helpful and courteous, and his companion attending to the luggage in a businesslike manner. I sat down in the carriage when we changed trains, thinking that I was getting towards the end of my journey now. Papa had told me that I would be met at Halifield station, and driven to Ditchford Hall.

We were passing through a number of little grey villages now. We went through a tunnel, and although I was not really nervous, there was something eerie about being the only woman in the darkness of the carriage. Mama would certainly not have approved — and yet, what harm was there?

The train leaped out into the daylight again, and I saw that the nature of the landscape was changing. Dry stone walls separated the fields; the trees were bent at an angle on the wide sweep of undulating moorland. Grey sheep cropped the grass at the foot of the hills.

I noticed the lambs seemed smaller than those I had seen in East Anglia — proof of a hard winter, and a bitter spring.

'How wild it is — and cruel looking,' I murmured, half to myself.

'Yes, but beautiful — beautiful with a wild, rugged grandeur.'

I was surprised at the enthusiasm in Mr. Stacey's voice. Evidently he loved this county, or he would not have defended it so warmly. Then the expression on his face changed, and took on a closed in, brooding look.

'Out on those moors in winter, a man could get caught in a storm, and die . . . '

I gave an involuntary shudder, and instantly he became apologetic.

'Do pardon me for saying that, Miss Meredith. Such talk is hardly pleasant for you to listen to. The Yorkshire countryside is beautiful, and I have no doubt you will enjoy your stay here.'

'I certainly hope so.'

There was a pause in the conversation. Mr. Stacey appeared to be turning something over in his mind.

'Did you mention the name of the family you were staying with?' he asked finally.

He knew perfectly well that I had

not; I felt embarrassed and unsure what to say.

'The name is Dewbrey,' I said slowly, and with some reluctance.

'Dewbrey!' he exclaimed, and to my surprise I saw him flush.

His travelling companion, who had been leaning back looking idly through the window, removed his gaze from the landscape, and gave me a sharp, searching glance.

'You have heard of them, then?' I asked.

Mr. Stacey recovered his composure. 'Yes, I have heard of them,' he said, speaking with a casualness which his eyes belied.

I glanced at my watch.

'You must be tired of travelling, Miss Meredith,' he went on. I smiled at him.

'I am, rather.'

'No doubt you will be met at Halifield station?'

'Oh, yes. Most certainly.'

He looked thoughtful again. 'It is rather surprising to find a young lady travelling alone such a distance.'

'I do surprising things,' I replied.

He looked at me without speaking, and Mr. Dryden remarked that we would be in Halifield in a few minutes. I tried to appear calm and unruffled, but inwardly I was a-tremble with nervousness.

'We will attend to your luggage — and get a porter if necessary,' he said gravely.

'Thank you, Mr. Dryden — you are both very kind.'

I put on my bonnet, aware that Hugh Stacey was watching me admiringly.

'Delightful,' he murmured. 'It has been a very pleasant journey.'

He was so gallant. I knew that I was going to miss him, although I had only known him a short time.

He and Mr. Dryden put the valises on the floor of the carriage as the train began to slow up. I drew a deep breath as the platform came into sight with a bare sprinkling of people on it.

I noticed two men standing together

as the train drew to a halt — a middle-aged man in grey livery, and a taller, younger one. Mr. Stacey opened the carriage door and helped me alight. Mr. Dryden handed the luggage out.

'You say you will be met . . . ' Hugh Stacey broke off. I glanced along the platform, and saw the two men I had noticed were looking around and were eyeing me.

'I can see your escort,' said Mr. Stacey. 'The dark gentleman over there, and a family retainer.'

The cold sarcasm in his voice startled me. The two men he had indicated exchanged a few words with each other, and began to walk in my direction.

'I have no excuse for staying with you any longer,' said Hugh quickly, his voice gentle again. 'Good day to you, Miss Meredith.'

He swept off his hat, and shook my hand. Mr. Dryden bowed without speaking, and they both turned away.

3

'Excuse me, madam, am I addressing Miss Meredith?'

The taller of the two men Mr. Stacey had described as my escort stood in front of me, while the other waited respectfully in the background.

'That is correct, sir.'

'I am Alec Dewbrey, and I have come from Ditchford Hall to meet you. Stubbs, take the young lady's baggage — I'll take this one.'

He replaced his hat, picked up one of the valises, and led the way out of the station, the liveried servant following with the rest of my luggage.

This Mr. Dewbrey had an authoritative manner, I thought. Was he the son of the house?

'This is the carriage, Miss Meredith.'

A fine pair of chestnut horses were standing in front of a smart brougham.

Stubbs loaded my baggage on, and I felt the pressure of Alec Dewbrey's hand on my arm as he helped me in. Just before I stepped inside I caught a glimpse of Hugh Stacey and his friend getting into a dogcart. So they were being driven home too.

My new travelling companion sat down opposite me, and the horses started off with a smart clip-clop.

How different Mr. Dewbrey was from Hugh Stacey. He was dark; olive-skinned, and so broad that he appeared to be almost bulging out of his suit, although this was not so really. I could see that it was no less well cut than Mr. Stacey's.

He had fine brown eyes, and, I thought, an arrogant looking mouth. I wondered why Hugh Stacey had hurried away like that, before Mr. Dewbrey had come up to see me. I put my hand to my forehead.

'Have you a headache, Miss Meredith?'

'A slight one.'

'It is scarcely surprising,' he said. 'No

doubt you will be glad to have a proper meal, and to refresh yourself after such a long journey. You will probably be wondering who I am . . . I am the late Mr. Dewbrey's nephew, and I manage Ditchford Hall estate for my aunt.'

I could not help thinking that the position became him well. How old would he be? I hazarded a guess that he was in his late twenties.

'Perhaps you could tell me more about Ditchford Hall, sir,' I suggested.

'It is quite a large place, situated a mile or so from Swalewell village. The house was built towards the end of the seventeenth century, since when Caldecotts have lived in it continuously.'

'Caldecotts?' I said. 'Has the house been bought from them, then?'

'My aunt's first husband was a Caldecott,' explained Alec Dewbrey. 'Unfortunately, like many old families, the Caldecotts have died out — no doubt my aunt will tell you more about it. To get back to the house itself — we are fortunate in having a very good staff of servants.'

'You are fortunate indeed,' I murmured.

He went on telling me about Ditchford Hall, and as I sat there, listening to this dark, masterful man, I was sure I could hear another set of hoofbeats along the road.

'Clip-clop, clip-clop, clip-clop, clip-clop . . . '

I strained my ears, wondering if Hugh Stacey was travelling along the same road. Suddenly Mr. Dewbrey stopped talking, and looked at me with a wry expression on his face.

'Yes, it is the Staceys' dogcart,' he said coolly. 'I have no doubt you found him an attentive companion on the train. When young ladies travel alone, they are, of course, open to annoying attentions from strangers.'

'I can assure you, sir,' I said indignantly, 'Mr. Stacey pressed no annoying attentions on me. He was my travelling companion for some time

— and it made the journey a great deal pleasanter for me than it would have been otherwise.'

'Indeed?'

The dark eyes were hard. 'As a travelling companion I do not propose to compete with the Stacey charm. However, I advise you to regard it as one of those episodes so dear to the hearts of romantic young ladies — in other words, put all thoughts of the debonair Mr. Stacey out of your mind.'

I felt like exploding at his presumptuousness. How arrogant he was — he knew well enough that I was to be little better than a servant in his aunt's house. Then why had he come personally to meet me, instead of just sending the coachman? I lapsed into a puzzled silence. It was misty now; the wind had dropped. Through the carriage window I could see hedgerows, and vague outlines of the undulating countryside.

Stubbs reined in the horses, and turned them onto a narrow lane winding upwards. The sound of the other set of hoofbeats died away. It seemed to get colder; I shivered slightly.

The mist was swirling around now, although it did not appear to worry the horses. Before long, though, they began to slacken their pace, and I realised we were at the gates of a lodge. A man holding a lantern exchanged a few words with the coachman; the gates were opened, and we were through them, and clip-clopping along the drive.

'Only a few minutes, now, Miss Meredith,' said Mr. Dewbrey, and his voice was surprisingly kind and solicitous. I wondered if perhaps he regretted his somewhat sarcastic manner of a short while before.

The horses drew to a standstill, and I knew we were there at last. Alec Dewbrey alighted, and offered me a helping hand. In the misty dusk of late afternoon I could see the house, overwhelmingly large and imposing. The coachman handed down my bags, and carried them up the steps to the entrance porch.

I could hear a dog barking from within, and the door was opened by a sober-faced man whom I judged to be a footman — or was he the butler?

A great mastiff dog leaped forward, barking, but Mr. Dewbrey silenced it with a word. Stubbs carried in my bags, touched his hat, and withdrew. I was in a vast, marble-floored hall, with a great open fire-place at one end.

'Is Mrs. Draycott available?' enquired Mr. Dewbrey of the manservant. 'She is needed, to attend to Miss Meredith — ah, here she is, to be sure.'

A middle-aged woman, plump, but dignified, appeared. She was dressed in black, relieved only by the white cap she wore.

'This is the housekeeper, Mrs. Draycott.' Mr. Dewbrey gave me an encouraging little smile as he spoke. 'This is Mrs. Dewbrey's companion, Miss Meredith. Will you show her to her room, and arrange for her to have a light meal before dinner is served.'

The housekeeper bowed slightly in my direction.

'Come this way, miss,' she said.

The lugubrious looking manservant picked up my luggage, except for the hatbox, which he handed me to carry. I followed Mrs. Draycott up the great carved staircase and along seemingly endless corridors, followed by the footman. At last she stopped and opened the door of what was evidently my room.

It was vast, in comparison with my bedroom at home, dominated by a huge four-poster bed, draped with heavy crimson curtains. The footman put my bags down, and withdrew without speaking. Although the room was large, it was warmly welcoming, with a glowing fire in the hearth. Mrs. Draycott lit the lamp on the bureau, and drew the curtains at the wide, lofty windows, shutting out the misty gloom.

My first impression was of the beauty of the mahogany furniture; the fire seemed to throw out a secondary warmth from its reflections in the wardrobe and dressing-table.

It's a lovely room — a luxurious room, I thought, excitement tingling through me.

'Is this room at the front of the house?' I enquired.

'Oh, yes, miss. The view is magnificent.'

She rang the bell, explaining that she was having hot water brought, and that she would send up some tea for me.

She then left me, saying that she had several things to attend to, but that she would be pleased to show me around, or tell me anything I wanted to know later that week.

I opened a valise and began to unpack it, but before long there was a gentle knock at the door.

'Mrs. Draycott said I had to bring hot water,' explained the attractive young maidservant standing there with a steaming ewer. She had round, solemn blue eyes.

'The mistress said if you needed any

help dressing, I was to offer my services. They call me Alice Byers.'

'Thank you, Alice. If you could help me with my toilet in the mornings — my hair particularly — I should be glad.'

She poured out the water for me, and without being asked, continued unpacking my things, very carefully.

'I'll wear that silk dress,' I said, taking my new, blue-green creation out of her hands. A few minutes later she deftly helped me into it, and I decided she was going to be very useful indeed.

* * *

She had unpacked my toilet things, and set them out on the dressing-table. She unpinned my straight, heavy hair, and brushed it with the silver-backed brush which I had bought myself out of my allowance from Papa.

'In future I shall probably have it done in ringlets,' I said.

'Yes, miss,' said Alice placidly, not realising that to me it was quite a landmark in my life. I looked at my reflection in the mirror. In my new dress, of which Mama had thoroughly disapproved, I decided nobody could look less like the daughter of a country parson.

Perhaps this fact should not have given me pleasure, but rightly or wrongly it did. Indeed, in the soft glow of the lamp, with Alice putting the last pin in my hair, I felt quite a great lady. Of course, I may not be Mrs. Dewbrey's idea of a companion at all, I told myself. But for my first meeting with her, I intended to look my best.

There was another knock at the door, and another maid, Ida, appeared, carrying a tray covered with a crisp, white, napkin.

'Dinner at eight, miss, in case Mrs. Draycott didn't tell you,' she said, putting down the tray. I thanked her, and both the maids withdrew. I took the napkin off the tray, to find wafer thin slices of bread and butter, tiny home-made scones, jam, and seed cake. There was tea in a small, silver teapot, with a matching sugar bowl and cream jug.

I sat down, poured out a cup of tea, and ate the dainty fare. Already it seemed an eternity since I had said goodbye to my parents and Emma.

I bit into a slice of seed cake, and wondered what Mrs. Dewbrey would expect of me. I reflected that life in Ditchford Hall could not be so terrible, or the maids would hardly be as contented looking and happy as they appeared to be.

4

Some time later there was a knock on the door. I opened it to find Alice standing there.

'The mistress would like to see you in her sitting-room before dinner is served,' she said.

'Very well, Alice,' I said, slipping a shawl round my shoulders. With a lighted candle in a silver candlestick, the girl led me down the corridor, our shadows waxing and waning in the dim light. She stopped and tapped on a door not very far from my own. She opened it, I walked forward, and it was closed silently behind me. I was alone in the presence of my employer.

My first impression of her, in the combined light of fire and lamp, was one of extreme elegance. She rose when I entered, and she was both tall and slender.

'Miss Deborah Meredith?'

I bowed and held out my hand, feeling overwhelmingly shy and nervous in spite of my new dress and careful toilet.

'I hope I see you well, ma'am.'

I felt her hand touch mine; she bowed her head while her eyes searched my face with an intense and disconcerting scrutiny. Her face was lined, but her bearing youthful; she was as upright as a girl. I thought she was probably in her late sixties — Mama had vaguely referred to her as being 'elderly'.

She sat down, and indicated that I should do so in the comfortable wing chair opposite her.

'I trust you had a good journey.'

'Very good, thank you, ma'am.'

After a slight pause, she asked if my parents were well.

'They are, and they send their regards,' I replied.

I had a curious feeling that politeness and nothing more had prompted this exchange of civilities between Mrs.

Dewbrey and my mother and father.

'Perhaps you will be kind enough to tell me what my duties will consist of,' I suggested.

I glanced round, and thought what a delightful room it was. It had an atmosphere of restfulness and charm which I found very attractive. There was a rosewood piano with sheets of music on top; I wondered if it was played very often.

'Yes, your duties, my dear. Such duties as I will give you may be deemed very light. In the mornings perhaps we will draw a little — or go out in the carriage if the weather is good. In the afternoons I rest, so you will be free every afternoon until tea time. In the evenings you may read aloud to me, or perhaps we may have some music. My nephew, Alec, plays the piano very well. He will join us sometimes, I expect.'

I sat there waiting, but Mrs. Dewbrey appeared to have finished speaking for the time being. The duties which she had outlined could have been performed by any well-brought-up young woman — or a much older woman, for that matter.

'We will have to arrange things later on, my dear. Quite often I retire early — although sometimes we entertain, but very quietly. It will be nice for Alec to have someone young — sometimes I scarcely feel like acting as hostess. There will be times when you will be more suitable.'

I sat there feeling astonished, and more than a little apprehensive. She was implying that sometimes I could act as hostess when Mr. Dewbrey entertained.

How could I possibly do that, a paid companion?

'Do you ride, Miss Meredith?'

'I am afraid not.'

'Then that is something you must learn. Do you dance?'

'I have been told I dance quite well,' I said, smiling.

My parents had not forbidden it, but

they had not encouraged it, either. However, Georgina and I had danced together quite often in her drawing-room, and I knew that I was reasonably proficient at it. The conversation continued; a rather odd one, as it consisted mainly of questions asked somewhat spasmodically by Mrs. Dewbrey, and of my replies. Nevertheless, by the time I had been in her company for an hour, she had managed to get a very fair picture of what my life at home had been like.

I stifled a yawn. We were sitting close to the fire, and the warmth made me feel drowsy, particularly during the periods when Mrs. Dewbrey sat pensively gazing into it.

The fireplace was of marble, with delicate porcelain figures on the mantelpiece. There was one small water-colour in a silver frame; a portrait of a young man, darkly handsome, with fine eyes.

'You are tired,' said Mrs. Dewbrey. 'I have asked you many questions. It must have been a long day for a young lady of some eighteen summers . . . '

She sat, deep in thought for a few minutes, then repeated, as if to herself: 'Some eighteen summers . . . '

At this point there was a tap at the door, and Alice announced that dinner was served.

'Sometimes I don't notice the time,' said Mrs. Dewbrey, rising slowly out of her chair.

Alice held the candle to light our way, and we followed her along the dark corridors, and down a wide flight of stairs.

'Tomorrow we will have to show you round the house and grounds,' went on my employer. 'You have, of course, met my nephew who manages the estate for me. No doubt he is already in the dining-room.'

She was right about this. Alice led us into a magnificent room, with a carved ceiling and a long table, bright with the glow of candles set in gleaming candelabra. Standing with his back to the huge log fire, a thoughtful expression on his face, was Alec Dewbrey.

'Good evening, Aunt Caroline,' he said. He advanced, and led her to the head of the table. The footman indicated a place for me on her left, and Mr. Dewbrey sat down on her right. Across the table his eyes met mine.

'I have been talking to Miss Meredith,' said his aunt conversationally, as the footman poured wine. 'She doesn't ride, Alec. She must be taught.'

'I'll make arrangements,' was his brief reply.

I said nothing, but the whole thing seemed to be taking on an unreal quality. I was unused to wine, but that first evening I was too nervous to refuse it. I sipped it cautiously, nevertheless I could feel it going to my head, just a little.

We had rabbit soup, fried soles, lamb cutlets and roast duckling, followed by charlotte russe and cheese straws. The solemn-faced footman who had somewhat grudgingly carried my bags to my room appeared more in his element serving dinner, assisted by a fresh faced young woman who was obviously the parlour maid.

'I will get the housekeeper to show you round the place,' said Mrs. Dewbrey. 'I will show you certain places, but I fear it is far too tiring for me to take you on a tour of the whole place. Perhaps Alec will show you the grounds — or at least, the parts I am unable to show you.'

'I shall be delighted,' said her nephew. I did not know if he was merely being polite, or if there was an edge of sarcasm in his voice. 'You are not acquainted with these parts at all, are you, Miss Meredith?' he went on.

'Not at all, sir. All I know of the West Riding are the things which are common knowledge.'

' 'The things which are common knowledge',' he repeated, a gleam of almost impish amusement appearing in his dark eyes. 'Pray tell me, what are these things, Miss Meredith?'

'Just that — well — Halifield is a busy trading town,' I said. 'I know there are mills here, and weaving and cloth manufacturers — and — er . . . '

'And that the Calder rises in the Pennines and flows windingly eastwards, and that it gives us the streams from whence we get our water power? Such facts are taught in the schoolroom, and are easily learned. Not so easily understood are the strange stubborn ways of the natives — the Yorkshire people who are born and live in these wild hills and valleys.'

'Anyone would think you didn't like living here,' said his aunt, in a mildly chiding tone. 'It's his adopted county — he lived in London until he was sixteen — and then when he came here he fell in love with it straight away,' she continued, talking to me. 'I don't know whether he classes himself with the natives or not.'

'I am a native,' I said quietly. 'I was born in Swalewell, although I know my parents left when I was scarcely a month old.'

To my surprise a look of deep sadness crossed Mrs. Dewbrey's face as I spoke. Her nephew looked quite startled; evidently she had not told him many details concerning her acquaintance with my parents.

He recovered his composure.

'You never told me that, Aunt Caroline,' he said good-naturedly. 'All that you said was that you knew Miss Meredith's parents years ago, and that you were sure she would make you an ideal companion.'

'And why not?' asked his aunt, adopting a rather flippant tone of voice as though she was trying to pass off his surprise with as little fuss as possible. 'After all, she should suit me. She is a native like myself — strange and stubborn, no doubt.'

Alec Dewbrey laughed.

'Time will show if that is true of Miss Meredith. I scarcely think it is true of you, Aunt Caroline.'

'Perhaps I had better say nothing on that subject,' said Mrs. Dewbrey. 'We all fall far short of perfection, I'm afraid. Don't you agree, Miss Meredith?'

The wine I had drunk made me feel quite bold.

'Indeed I do. I have found people to be strange and stubborn without being Yorkshire.'

Amusement gleamed in his eyes, and something else, something not so easily defined. Probably he thought me a pert miss; certainly I had not accepted his somewhat scathing remarks concerning Hugh Stacey.

I had tried to imagine what life would be like at Ditchford Hall; I now saw that it was going to be different from anything I had thought. And yet, it was going to be a challenge.

Not least would be the challenge of living in daily contact with this rather baffling man, who could be sarcastic and arrogant, and yet kind and friendly too, with eyes which twinkled merrily when he was amused.

'Very often we don't use the drawing room in the evenings; I usually go to my sitting-room, and Alec joins me there if he has a mind,' explained Mrs. Dewbrey. 'I shall go there in a few minutes. You may sit with me if you wish, Miss Meredith, or you may prefer to go straight to your room. Doubtless you have things to do.'

I was grateful to her for this thoughtfulness. We left the table together, and Alec Dewbrey remained alone in the dining-room.

In future I would drink water with my dinner, not wine, I decided when at last I was alone in my room.

I undressed straight away, putting my treasured silk dress away carefully. If only Hugh Stacey could see me in it . . . I thought sleepy, delightful thoughts, remembering the admiration in his eyes. I climbed into bed; it was soft and comfortable, and roomy enough to lie crossways if I chose. In spite of so many different thoughts whirling through my head, I must have fallen asleep quickly, only to be roused from my slumber in a strange and frightening manner.

I thought that I was dreaming — dreaming that someone was bending over me and kissing me. I had left my bed curtains undrawn as I always did; something brushed against my forehead so softly, so swiftly, that it was like being touched by a butterfly.

With a start I opened my eyes, and in the faint glimmer of the firelight I saw a figure leaving the room.

For a moment I thought that I was still dreaming, then I saw the visitor slip out of the door, and disappear silently.

I sat up in bed, startled and frightened, jerked wide awake by what I had seen. Someone had entered my room and kissed me!

In spite of the warmth and cosiness of the big four-poster bed, I shivered.

Although I had just had time to discern that there was a presence in my bedchamber, I had not had time to see who the intruder was. It was no dream, though, for I had heard the faint sound of my bedroom door being closed very quietly.

My heart was pounding. I slipped out of bed, and crept towards the door. Opening it, I peered out into the passage, but there was only darkness and silence. Trembling, I turned the key in the lock, and secured the door.

Who had entered and left my room so silently that it was a wonder I had wakened at all?

The fire was nearly out, but my eyes had grown accustomed to the darkness now. I looked fearfully round, but there was no presence save my own. I walked over to the window, and made sure that it was securely closed. I then climbed back into bed.

For the rest of the night I would be free from unwelcome visitors at all events. Knowing this did not make me fall asleep any more readily though, in spite of my tiredness. For a long time I lay there, listening. The wind had risen, and occasionally the window gave a slight rattle.

I longed for the night to be over, and

for the darkness to go. When I did fall asleep it was to dream of Hugh Stacey.

Nor was it a pleasant dream — I dreamt that we were hand in hand, running somewhere and being pursued. The figure of a man appeared in front of us — I screamed in my sleep — and woke with a start to the sound of knocking on my door.

I was sticky with perspiration; my first night at Ditchford Hall had not been a good one. I remembered my door was locked, and hastily putting on a wrapper, I opened it to admit Alice Byers, placid and round-faced, bearing a ewer of hot water.

'Good day, Alice.'

'Good day, miss. I forgot to mention it yesterday, but tell me when you want a bath. I'll see to it for you.'

She entered my room, and drew back the curtains. I picked up my watch from the bureau, and was surprised to see it was after eight o'clock.

'It's been a wild night,' said Alice companionably, pouring the water into the washbasin. 'Which dress shall I put out, miss?'

She was a nice girl. True, when she spoke her accent was harsh and ugly, but she was so honest looking, so down-to-earth, and so neat and pretty that for a moment I nearly confided in her. But something held me back. Servants tittle-tattled, even the best of them, and stories of being kissed in the night by unseen visitors were not the sort of things one wants repeating below stairs.

I selected a simple, grey morning dress, and Alice helped me into it.

'The mistress has breakfast in her room,' she told me. 'She never rises before ten o'clock. I thought 'appen you wouldn't want to be as late as that.'

'You are quite right, I wouldn't,' I said, taking pleasure in sitting in front of the mirror while Alice brushed my hair. 'Usually I rise earlier than this. I must have been very tired.'

'When you want me in the mornings, just ring the bell, miss,' said Alice. 'Or I'll come every morning at eight if you like. Later on I help the mistress dress.'

So I was sharing Mrs. Dewbrey's maid. With deft hands she pinned up my hair.

'Tell me when you want ringlets, miss, and I'll bring the tongs with me.'

I felt quite a glow of importance. When Alice had finished, I looked through the window at the magnificent view beyond. The long drive was tree-lined, with a wide sweep of parkland on either side. Close to the house were terraces and lawns, with daffodils and primulas already making a brave splash of colour in the flower beds.

'It's a beautiful place, miss,' said Alice, following my gaze. 'Do you know your way down to the breakfast-room?'

'Not yet,' I said. 'I shall have to learn my way about in Ditchford Hall.'

'I'll show you the way, then.'

I followed Alice's trim figure along the corridors and down the wide staircase.

5

I thought the breakfast-room was beautiful; it contained superb furniture and had a white marble fireplace decorated with a frieze of *putti*. As in the other rooms there was a big, welcoming fire.

Alice rang the bell.

'The cold dishes are on the sideboard, miss,' she said. 'Ella will bring in the rest.'

She withdrew, and I allowed myself the luxury of staring round the room. Sombrely beautiful oil paintings adorned the walls; I imagined most of them were family portraits. I glanced up at the rococo ceiling, and thought of the long hours of labour such exquisite craftsmanship must have required.

The parlourmaid appeared bearing a tray containing coffee, hot rolls, bacon and eggs.

'There's game pie and a ham on the sideboard, miss,' she said.

'Thank you, I prefer something hot,' I told her.

She set out the food, and then deftly attended to the fire.

'Am I the only one to breakfast?' I enquired.

'Yes, miss. Mr. Alec breakfasted earlier.'

I ate my solitary meal, and afterwards stood at the window, looking out across the sweep of parkland. Everywhere seemed so peaceful, so secure. The pale spring sun slipped out from behind a cloud, and transformed the scene into one of rare loveliness.

And yet, in spite of the atmosphere of peace and serenity, the fear which I had felt during the night still lingered. Someone had entered my bedroom and kissed me. But who?

Not the glum-faced footman, surely. A feeling of distaste rose in me. Not Alec Dewbrey; to my annoyance I could feel myself flushing. Tonight I would lock my door straight away, and make sure the window was securely fastened.

'Good morning, miss,' said a voice, and Mrs. Draycott came into the room, her black gown swishing importantly. 'I'll show you round the house until the mistress is ready.'

As we left the breakfast-room she asked if I had slept well that night. For a moment I hesitated.

'One never does really — I never seem to sleep very well the first night in a strange bed,' I replied. 'Now I suppose you are going to tell me the place is haunted.'

Mrs. Draycott smiled. 'I've never heard so. I've been here these past seven years, and never seen owt like that. Anyway, it's not the dead that hurts you, miss. It's t' living.'

We were in the entrance hall now.

'I can't tell you all the details like the mistress can, or Mr. Alec. But the main part of the house was built about a hundred and fifty years ago — I think. Of course, a lot has been added on . . . '

She broke off while I gazed up and down.

'And this is the rose drawing-room,' she said, a few minutes later.

'It's beautiful,' I said, looking at the superb ceiling, from which hung a lovely crystal chandelier.

'I believe the pictures here are Italian and worth a great deal. All the Caldecotts have been art collectors and the like.'

'The Caldecotts?' I exclaimed.

'Yes. I never knew any of 'em, but it's the Caldecotts' place. Mrs. Tukes, the cook — she's been here over thirty years — she knows all about the family. Mr. Charles Caldecott was the mistress's first husband — he died, and a good many years later she married Mr. Dewbrey.'

'And I suppose he came to live here, then?' I asked musingly, following her out of the rose drawing-room.

'Aye — he died too, about a year after I came. Quiet gentleman — I think they had tastes in common. He was happen a comfort to her. She had a son, but she lost him years ago. She's had her share of trouble — you'll have seen the dining-room?'

'Yes,' I said, glancing again at the sombre magnificence of the sideboards, the wine coolers, and the urn pedestals.

We walked up the handsome oak staircase, and Mrs. Draycott led me into the upper drawing-room, which was long and narrow.

'That clock's a hundred and fifty years old, miss. And of course, more pictures. Some of them were painted by the mistress. She and Mr. Dewbrey both used to paint and sketch, and the like.'

As I looked round I was attracted by an oil painting which I felt sure portrayed the same young man as I had noticed in water colour in Mrs Dewbrey's sitting-room.

'She didn't paint that. They say it cost a deal to have it done — that's him — her son — Mr. Will, as the old servants call him. I never knew him, of course. Come on, I'll show you the tapestry room . . . there, isn't it a treat?'

The tapestries looked as fresh in colour as though they had just been done, harmonising perfectly with the gold-and-needlework chairs, the carpet, and the fine plasterwork of the ceiling.

We passed on to the sculpture gallery, consisting of three linked rooms joined by vaulted arches.

Everywhere I could see evidence that people of taste had lived in this house for generations, and left their indelible stamp upon it.

'And this is the library,' said Mrs. Draycott, opening another door. 'Oh, I beg your pardon, sir,' she added, dropping a slight curtsey. 'I didn't think anyone would be in this time o' morning. I'm showing Miss Meredith around.'

Alec Dewbrey was sitting at a desk with a pile of books in front of him.

'Pray continue, then,' he said, with a bland smile in my direction. 'Good day, Miss Meredith. I see you have survived your first night at Ditchford Hall.'

'Yes, thank you,' I replied, hoping I was not blushing.

The memory of that kiss was very fresh in my mind. I glanced round the room, and liked it straight away. Tempting looking books lined the walls, and the leather chairs looked comfortable and well used. Mrs. Draycott closed the door quietly, and we left him to his business.

'Mr. Alec has plenty to do. Of course Dan Tulloch helps him . . . I'll show you my part of the house. I have my own room, and I get my meals in it. I don't go int' Servants' Hall. Mr. Crowther has his meals with me — the butler died last year after twenty years here — Mr. Crowther reckons to be the butler now. And Stainthorpe, the footman — well, he's a young nowt, if you ask me. He calls himself Mr. Alec's valet . . . '

She chattered on, and led me into the kitchen, where I met the cook, Mrs. Tukes, with two of the maids. She was a tall, grey-haired, quiet woman.

'Good morning, miss,' she said, smiling pleasantly. Then suddenly, her face changed. She looked startled; surprise, bewilderment, and like emotions crossed her placid features.

'I can see you're very busy,' I said, as I felt bound to say something. As we left the kitchen I could feel her eyes following me. Mrs. Draycott, however, appeared to have noticed nothing untoward.

'I think the mistress will be in her sitting-room now,' she said, after conducting me around for another quarter of an hour. 'She may want to show you the grounds and gardens herself. Happen you'll be able to find your way around the place a bit better now.'

'Yes, I think so. Thank you for showing me around.'

The housekeeper went off silently. There was no doubting her efficiency; large as it was, the house seemed to run with enviable smoothness. No doubt

'Mr. Alec' played his part, I reflected, thinking of him busy in the library. I supposed the servants had called him that while his uncle was alive, and had found the habit hard to drop.

Mrs. Dewbrey was sitting in front of the fire, her feet on a hassock. She was dressed in grey, with a fringed silk shawl over her shoulders.

'Good day, my dear. I trust you slept well.'

'Good day, ma'am. I slept very well.'

This was not true, but I had decided not to mention my night experience to anyone.

'Mrs. Draycott has been showing me around the house.'

'And do you like what you see?'

Mrs. Dewbrey indicated a chair opposite her.

'Yes, the rooms are very lovely. The whole house is lovely.'

A rather sad expression crossed her face, and then she said:

'I'm glad you like it. I should like to show you the gardens myself.'

'Certainly — whenever you please,' I said.

'There is another matter before that, though. I shall be paying you quarterly, and I would like to give you a quarter's payment in advance. You must have a riding habit made as soon as possible — and any other clothes which are necessary.'

'Thank you, ma'am, but I have enough clothes to last me for a while,' I replied uncertainly.

'There is a very good dressmaker in Halifield,' she went on, as if she had not heard me. I was about to speak, but checked myself. It occurred to me that this lady was very rich, and also rather eccentric.

She handed me a sealed envelope.

'I have put your quarterly pay in here. Now let us go out into the garden until luncheon. Tell me, my dear, have you left many friends behind in Norfolk?'

I had already mentioned Georgina to her.

'Not a great many,' I said. 'My family took up a good deal of my time.'

'You did not meet any young gentlemen, of course?'

Although she spoke casually, her eyes betrayed keen interest. I wondered why.

'Not a great many,' I replied.

I might have added: 'And certainly none who appealed to me,' but decided that was scarcely called for. Besides, I had met Hugh Stacey, and what might have been true two days before no longer applied.

'Ring for Alice to bring my cloak,' she said, after we had been sitting together for about half an hour. I went to my room to get mine, and we started off at a slow pace round the grounds. The sun peeped out again, and I took deep breaths of the spring air.

Mrs. Dewbrey became quite animated, drawing my attention to the beautifully trimmed hedges and the impressive stone and lead statues standing on the lawn. It was plain that she loved every inch of the place, even though she herself was not a Caldecott.

Standing away from the house I admired the fine façade, with its mullioned windows. We proceeded slowly; it was some time before she showed me the greenhouses, and I met Tresset, the head gardener. He was a man in his middle fifties, and had been at Ditchford Hall all his working life. He seemed to be peering at me too, or was it my imagination? I decided it must be.

Dick, his tousle-haired young assistant, gave me a crookedly winning smile. Another man was busy in the background.

'I spend hours in the walled garden in the summer months,' Mrs. Dewbrey informed me. 'I think you will like it.'

She led me through a delightful orchard to the garden beyond. It was beautifully laid out, with many plants beginning to bud up. There were daffodils and wallflowers in bloom; clematis, ivy, and other creepers clung to the old wall, and there was a lawn with a sundial in the centre.

There were seats round the lawn at intervals. The high stone wall protected us from the fresh breeze, which, Mrs. Dewbrey told me 'swept straight down from the moors'.

'You haven't seen the stables yet,' she said.

'I can have a look round myself — perhaps when you are resting, ma'am,' I suggested.

'Certainly. You are at liberty to do that, Miss Meredith. The stables are over there — part of the west wing, really.'

She indicated the buildings. 'The grounds extend right over to the river — Swalewell Beck. I never go down there.'

She spoke the last words with indescribable sadness in her voice. I made up my mind to explore further by myself, as soon as I found the opportunity. We walked slowly back to the house.

The fresh air had sharpened my

appetite, and I found myself looking forward to luncheon.

'Ah, good day Alec,' exclaimed Mrs. Dewbrey, when we met in the dining-room shortly afterwards. There was no mistaking the affection in her voice.

He greeted her with solicitous protectiveness in his; undoubtedly they were on good terms with each other.

'No doubt you have been showing Miss Meredith round,' he said. 'I hope you have not tired yourself too much.'

'Not at all. We have not been able to look at everything, of course. I thought you might show Miss Meredith the stables, Alec.'

'I will certainly do so at the earliest opportunity.' His dark eyes turned on me.

'Thank you, sir,' I replied. I could feel my colour rising under his steady gaze. His mastiff dog, Horatio, was looking at me too. With a curiously stealthy movement he rested his great head on my knee, when we were seated. A little nervously I patted him, and he wagged his tail with delight.

'He's your slave for ever, Miss Meredith,' said Mr. Dewbrey lightly, and then he bade the dog lie down, lest it should make a nuisance of itself.

Luncheon was served, and although it was an excellent meal, I still felt rather shy having my food served in such grand surroundings with people who were virtually strangers.

'I shall retire to my room after luncheon,' Mrs. Dewbrey announced. 'Perhaps you wish to write letters, Miss Meredith.'

'Yes, I expect my family will be anxious to hear from me,' I said. 'Where will I have to go to post the letters?'

'If you put them on the table in the hall, someone will be going into the village this afternoon,' said Mrs. Dewbrey. 'Be sure you put them out before three o'clock.'

'Thank you. I shall certainly have them ready for that time,' I said.

'As soon as the spring comes, all the

tasks which need doing after the winter present themselves,' remarked Mr. Dewbrey 'I shall have to see Tulloch about mending the roof of the boat-house . . . '

He broke off abruptly, and Mrs. Dewbrey went on with her meal as though she had not heard him.

'Daisy's foal is coming along beautifully,' he said, just a little hastily. 'I'm sure Miss Meredith is going to spoil him outrageously when she sees him.'

His eyes sought mine almost anxiously.

'I'm sure I shall,' I murmured.

For the rest of the meal he discussed details of the estate with Mrs. Dewbrey, occasionally drawing me into the conversation. Afterwards she went to rest in her room, and I hurried off to mine. I had slipped the envelope she had given me into the top drawer of my dressing-table. I now took it out and opened it. Involuntarily I gave a little gasp, as gold coins slipped out onto my hand.

A quarter's pay! There were twenty gold sovereigns — I had not expected anything like that amount. I sat down, feeling bewildered. I was to have new clothes, Mrs. Dewbrey had said — and riding lessons. I had the services of a maid; I was surrounded by luxury and elegance — as for my duties — well, apart from playing the piano, and other pleasant diversions, they mostly appeared to be giving an old lady an interest in her declining years. But why?

Why had I been specially chosen for all this? I wondered what part my parents had played in it. If she thought so highly of them as to offer their daughter all these advantages, why did she hardly mention them when I told her about my life at the vicarage? I wrote a letter home, and one to Georgina.

I then put on my warm cape, with the intention of having a walk round the grounds by myself. I walked past the greenhouses and caught sight of Dick, who grinned knowingly. The lovely parkland stretched all around; how pleasant to be the owner of such well-kept land, I thought. I saw the river, then, through the trees. There was a wooden building on the bank, dark and weathered looking.

I guessed this was the boathouse which needed some repairing, and walked down the bank to have a closer look. To my surprise the place was not empty; there was a man busily engaged in doing something to a rowing boat.

'Oh!' I gasped, rather taken aback.

'Well, miss! You give us a fright!'

He straightened up, and eyed me curiously. He was a big man, probably in his sixties, but rosy-cheeked and keen-eyed.

'I'm sorry. I walked round to have a look, and didn't expect to find someone busy. I'm Mrs. Dewbrey's companion, Miss Meredith.'

He nodded. 'Aye — I guessed that. I've heard tell of you. I'm Dan Tulloch, and I've been with the Caldecotts ever since I was a boy — and my father before me.'

He lit a pipe.

'I look after things, miss,' he went on. 'I keep my eye on the river, and thereabouts, and help Mr. Alec.'

'You will no doubt have seen many changes,' I said.

'Many changes. Many strange things, too.'

For a moment his eyes seemed to look into the past.

'And you're busy doing repair work,' I said.

'I like to keep everything in order, miss, whether it's in use or not.'

'I love boats,' I said impulsively.

'The young master loved the river. I used to take him out as a little boy . . . '

He broke off, and for a moment his eyes were looking into the past.

They veered round to me again. He passed his hand across his forehead.

'The light plays queer tricks,' he muttered.

'I'm going for a walk along the bank,' I said.

'Aye — well, don't walk any further than that high hedge, miss.'

'And who lives opposite? I can see a big house through the trees,' I said, nodding towards the bank at the other side of the river.

'That? That's Swalewell Keep,' he said slowly, almost as if he were speaking to himself. 'Aye, it's t'Keep — and the Staceys live there.'

6

A thrill of excitement and surprise shot through me at his words.

'Aye — the Staceys,' he repeated. I thought he was about to say more about them, but he appeared to change his mind.

'I live in that cottage along there, miss.' He pointed upstream, and in the distance I could see it. Also a dog, running from the direction of his house to where we were.

'My dog, Keeper,' he explained, just before a sturdy, wildly barking Airedale bore down upon us. Smiling, I left them both on the landing stage. I wanted to explore this place for myself — I wanted to go on the river, too, and I saw no reason why I should not take a rowing boat out. There were two in the boathouse. I decided I would see Tulloch about this in the near future.

I followed the river round, keeping a curious eye on the Staceys' side. I could see the house more clearly now, even though it was half hidden by trees.

It had a tower and battlements — why, it was a castle!

Instinctively I knew that it was old; far older than Ditchford Hall. The very name, Swalewell Keep, revealed its ancient origin. It looked tremendously remote and impressive, but romantic, too.

I walked along the bank, noticing that it was well wooded on both sides, but more so on the Staceys' land.

The grounds of the Hall were even more extensive than I had thought; the hedge which Dan Tulloch had mentioned was still a good walk away. I caught a glimpse of a grey squirrel in a tree; the bob-tail of a rabbit scurried across my path. At last I reached the hedge. It was thick and high, but peeping round it, I could see a house further down the river, on the Staceys' land.

It was a poor looking place, a tumbledown cottage, set almost perilously close to the water's edge. I wondered who lived there.

I turned round and walked back to the Hall, where I took afternoon tea with Mrs. Dewbrey, in her sitting-room.

'Now tell me what you have been doing, my dear,' she said.

'I've written some letters, and had a good look round,' I said, pouring out the tea, as she had requested.

'I've been down to the river, I've seen the boathouse and met Dan Tulloch — Mrs. Dewbrey, are you ill?'

Her face looked pinched and grey, her lips faintly bluish.

'My medicine,' she said huskily, pointing to a bottle on the top of a china cabinet.

'How much do you need?' I asked, feeling very nervous, and not sure whether to ring for help or not. I watched her anxiously as she sipped it from a teaspoon, and swallowed a mouthful of tea. She lay back on the chintz covered chair, looking suddenly frail and old.

'Please tell me if I can do anything further, ma'am,' I said. She shook her head, indicating with a movement of her hand that I should carry on with my tea. After a few minutes she spoke again.

'I have these attacks sometimes, Miss Meredith. The doctor keeps an eye on me, and tells me not to overdo things.'

It crossed my mind that perhaps I would have to be something of a nurse as well as a companion. I thought again of the sovereigns which had fallen into my hand from the envelope she had given me. It was my duty to give of my services to the best of my ability.

'Perhaps you would like to rest while I play something,' I suggested.

'Yes, I would like that, my dear.'

I sat down at the lovely rosewood piano and began to play. I knew that I was no more than a competent pianist, but I loved music, and practising had never been a penance to me. I played from the sheet of music which was already out — a sweet, haunting air. As I sat there, with Mrs. Dewbrey listening, I had the most curious sense of belonging; for a few moments there seemed to be neither past nor present, and the feeling of being a stranger went too.

* * *

It was my first Sunday at Ditchford Hall, and Mrs. Dewbrey, her nephew and I were being driven through Swalewell village to church. It was a fine spring morning; I had my hair in ringlets which I thought were well set off by the grey bonnet I was wearing.

'Those buildings you can see over there are mills,' explained Mr. Dewbrey, seeing me glance curiously around.

'It's a very varied landscape,' I said slowly.

'Up to a point. Mills clinging to the river banks, stone cottages, and long Yorkshire farmhouses. Steep hills, and then valleys, and the village perched on the hillside. And then the church and parsonage, and beyond that . . . ' He broke off.

'And beyond that, Alec?' prompted his aunt.

'Beyond that the moors; solitude, space — only the wild creatures for company.'

'Papa told me about Swalewell church,' I said. 'He told me it was built by the Normans, and that it contains an effigy of a knight in the sanctuary.'

'Quite correct,' said Mr. Dewbrey, smiling. 'It is an interesting old place — it still has a Norman window in the north wall, although parts have been rebuilt. We are in Swalewell now.'

I looked round, and glimpsed the village green with its stone cross. As we proceeded up the cobbled main street, we passed an inn with the sign up: 'The Brown Cow'. The horses slowed down. It was a pull for them all the way, but they appeared used to it. We turned off into a lane just before the straggling cottages ended, and I saw the square tower of Swalewell village church. Mr. Dewbrey helped us both down from the carriage.

Just as we had alighted, a gay voice said: 'Good day to you, Mrs. Dewbrey — and to you, sir!'

I turned to see an incredibly beautiful and elegant young lady.

I was suddenly overwhelmingly aware that I was a paid companion, the daughter of a country clergyman, and that my clothes had been made by a village dressmaker.

Alec Dewbrey stood with his hat in his hand, and smiled at the enchanting vision. She was with an older lady, and they both glanced politely, but questioningly in my direction.

'This is my companion, Miss Deborah Meredith,' explained Mrs. Dewbrey, before her nephew had time to speak. 'This is Mrs. Campion and her daughter, Miss Penelope. They are friends of ours, and often come to the Hall.'

I bowed, feeling at a disadvantage. The younger lady, although smiling politely, gave me a much keener glance than she had done hitherto. Then her eyes went back to Alec Dewbrey's face.

She loves him, I thought. Her gay, friendly greeting could have been the sort any young lady might bestow on a gentleman of her acquaintance, but somehow I knew straight away that there was more to it than that. We walked through the windswept churchyard with its listing tombstones, and entered the austerely beautiful little church. I knelt down and tried to pray, but as so often happened, I found it difficult. When I was seated I glanced round, and saw Hugh Stacey sitting in a pew on the other side of the aisle. He was looking at me — he must have been in church first, and had seen me arrive. On one side of him sat an elderly grey-haired man who looked neither to right nor left as he sat there, and on the other side, Mr. Dryden.

To my annoyance I saw Mr. Dewbrey looking at me out of the corner of his eye. He had seen the glance between myself and Hugh Stacey. I looked straight ahead, and felt my cheeks burning.

The service began, reminding me poignantly of the services my father conducted in the village church at home. My attention soon wandered though — how elegant Hugh Stacey looked in his dark suit! At least I was sure of seeing him every Sunday. Then I fell to thinking of Miss Campion, whose blue eyes had looked at Mr. Dewbrey with such admiration. Some day he would marry, and Ditchford Hall would be his, I presumed. True, he was only a nephew by marriage, but to whom else would Mrs. Dewbrey leave all her property and possessions?

With a start I realised the service was ending.

We walked slowly out of the dimness of the church into the chilly brightness of the spring sunshine. Just as we were about to get into our carriage, Hugh Stacey appeared at the gates of the churchyard. He looked straight at me, and I could feel myself colouring up. Without glancing at my companions, he removed his hat, bowed, and with a swift 'Good day, Miss Meredith,' he strode away, followed by Mr. Dryden and the older man.

'Have you made the acquaintance of that young gentleman?' Mrs. Dewbrey enquired stiffly, when we were in the carriage.

'He was my travelling companion for part of the journey here, ma'am,' I explained demurely. I could feel disapproval coming from her. Mr. Dewbrey looked out of the window, and said nothing. I had the feeling he disapproved as strongly as his aunt. If only I dare ask outright why this curious enmity towards the Staceys!

As no one seemed talkative on the journey back, I fell to thinking about taking the rowing boat out. I made up my mind to see Dan Tulloch about it.

As soon as a riding habit was obtained for me, I had my first riding lesson. Mr. Dewbrey himself took me down to the stables one morning. Although I had been looking forward to it, I felt slightly apprehensive, too. The feeling soon left me, though; it was so interesting being shown around the place by John Stubbs. I saw the coach house, and the harness room, and learnt that the groom slept over the stables, and that the breed of the splendid carriage horses was called the Cleveland Bay.

'And there's none better in the world, miss. They can carry sixteen stones sixteen miles within an hour.'

Mr. Dewbrey laughed. 'We want a horse that can carry Miss Meredith, Stubbs. I want her to have riding lessons — either from you or the groom.'

'Why, yes, sir . . . and talking of the Cleveland Bay, have you seen Daisy's foal lately?'

'Not for a few days — I've been rather busy. We must show him to Miss Meredith.'

John Stubbs led us to where a soft-eyed chestnut mare stood licking a slender, appealing foal.

'Oh, he's beautiful!' I cried. 'I wish I'd brought a lump of sugar or something to give him!'

I caressed his silky head, and he nuzzled into me, while his mother looked indulgently on.

'We haven't thought of a name yet,' said John Stubbs. 'We'll have to be giving him one, sir.'

'His eyes look as though they are full of tears,' I said. 'Misty-eyed . . . why not call him Misty?'

'Why not, indeed?' Mr. Dewbrey was smiling. 'I think that's a capital name, Miss Meredith. Don't you, Stubbs?'

'Capital, sir. We haven't had a Misty in the stables before.'

Mr. Dewbrey gave the foal a last pat, and straightened up.

'You must excuse me now, Miss

Meredith. I must see Tulloch about something. You will be able to make arrangements for these lessons when it is convenient.'

He inclined his head in my direction, and went off with long, swinging strides. Somehow, without him, I felt shy and awkward, standing there in my neat, blue, riding habit.

'I think you'll soon take to it, miss. I'll put a side-saddle on Pansy, and walk you up and down a bit. Daisy and Pansy are both as gentle as lambs.' Stubbs chuckled. 'If Mr. Alec asks you how you fared, tell him you were riding Sorrel.'

'Sorrel?' I asked.

'Nay, miss, I'm just joking. Sorrel's a villain — I've told Mr. Alec that horse'll be the death of both of us.'

From the harness room he brought a side-saddle, and helped me to mount an amiable looking grey mare. With a leading rein in his hand, he walked beside me round the paddock, and I soon gained confidence and began to enjoy it.

'You've got the makings of a horsewoman, miss,' he said, after half an hour. I felt a sense of achievement, even though I knew I had a long way to go yet.

Later that week it became very hot for early May, and I decided to tackle Dan Tulloch about taking a boat out. One sunny afternoon I met him not far from the river, with Keeper at his heels. I broached the subject when we were near the boathouse.

'Well, miss, I don't know about that,' he said cautiously. 'It's dangerous beyond a certain point — there's a weir further down. There's a clump of trees — and that's as far as it's safe to go. Nay, I can't tek responsibility in letting you go.'

'But I shouldn't go beyond the clump of trees,' I said earnestly. 'I assure you, you can trust me.'

He stood shaking his head, but I had a feeling that he was weakening.

'You'll have to do all the steering with

the oars — nay, it's out o' t'question.'

'Are the boats in good order?' I enquired.

'Yes — and the landing stage. I'll tell you what. You row me down the river, and if I'm satisfied I'll row you back, and maybe you can take it out yourself tomorrow. But mind you're careful.'

'I'll be careful,' I promised.

'Have you told the mistress about wanting to go on the river?' asked Tulloch. Naturally, I had not.

'Mrs. Dewbrey does not mind how I occupy my afternoons,' I said coolly. He grunted, and proceeded to get one of the boats out into the water. Without saying anything further, he helped me into it, where I sat in the forward thwart, with him in the centre. I took the oars, while Keeper watched sullenly from the landing stage.

'It isn't usual for young ladies to row,' Tulloch observed, his voice disapproving.

'I have two brothers,' I replied, smiling. I could see him watching my handling of the oars as I brought the blades flat to the surface of the water, feathering neatly during the return stroke. We went smoothly down the stream and my passenger relaxed visibly. I had learnt to row when quite young during our summer holidays, and it was a thing I had always enjoyed doing.

'Who owns this stretch of river?' I enquired.

'T' Dewbreys,' was the brusque reply.

'These people who live at Swalewell Keep,' I said casually, 'The Staceys — are there many of them?'

'Nay, there's noan many.'

Tulloch was plainly not a gossip, and it would never do for me to appear vulgarly curious about the Staceys, even though I was.

'Shall I take the oars, now, miss?' asked Tulloch, when we were within sight of the clump of trees he had mentioned.

'There's no need,' I answered, turning the boat round. 'I'm not tired — and it saves changing over.'

'Very well, miss.'

I thought that I was handling the boat and the old retainer very well. Back at the landing stage I moored the boat securely, tying it with a clove-hitch under Tulloch's watchful eye.

'I can take it out sometimes in the afternoons, can't I?'

'Well, I can't see any reason why not. You seem to frame all right with it . . . ' He still looked uneasy, though, as if he felt no good would come of it. I gave him a cheerful smile, and set off back to the Hall. Although I felt pleased about many things concerning my new life, I still had pangs of homesickness.

Living away from home required getting used to, and there was no doubt I missed my family. Fortunately, time did not hang on my hands at Ditchford Hall. Both indoors and outdoors there was much to do. As for my riding, so swiftly did I gain skill and confidence in the saddle that Mr. Dewbrey rode with me into the village after the first few lessons.

7

It was an enjoyable experience. He was not mounted on the fearsome Sorrel, but on Aztec, a fine Cleveland Bay, while I rode the gentle Pansy. It was sunny, although cooler than it had been, with a strong breeze.

'I suppose Swalewell Beck runs right through the village,' I said.

'Yes — it is dangerous lower down where the weir is. They used to duck witches in the Beck in bygone days. It's not very wide, but quite deep.'

'I would like to have a really good look round the church, and see that effigy of a knight in the sanctuary. I wonder who built the church — some forgotten Norman, I suppose.'

He paused before replying.

'A Stacey built it,' he said finally. 'And the effigy is believed to be one Roger de Stacie — in those days it was spelt S-t-a-c-i-e — the name became Anglicised.'

I sensed that he had no desire to enlarge on that remark, so I did not pursue the subject.

'You were born in Swalewell, I believe?' he said, after we had ridden in silence for some time. We were going through the village now.

'Yes — in the curate's house.'

'It's over there,' he said, pointing with his riding crop. We slowed down while I looked.

It was just a grey stone house, indistinguishable from the others in the row; a modest dwelling, plain and solidly built.

'I must write and tell my parents I've seen it,' I said, feeling an unaccountable sadness as I looked at it.

He suggested that we should turn off by Swalewell church, if I would care for a closer look at it. We dismounted, and he tethered the horses outside the churchyard.

'The roof is of slate, fastened with

sheep-shank bones,' he said, before we entered the building. 'The Norman window in the north wall has been blocked from the inside, but the nave retains its original west door. The eastern end of the church was rebuilt in the fourteenth century . . . '

His voice dropped to a whisper as we went inside. Impersonally, efficiently, he showed me the empty building, drawing my attention to the tablets commemorating various Caldecotts who had been buried there. Most impressive of all was the effigy of the knight in the sanctuary, the equipment dating it as being thirteenth century.

This was no Caldecott, but an early forbear of Hugh Stacey's — a de Stacie of long ago, beautifully and skilfully carved, his feet resting on a mutilated beast with a knotted tail. On the walls of the nave hung various funeral achievements, including hatchments, standards, swords and gauntlets.

'Have the Staceys a vault?' I asked in a whisper.

'It's been blocked up,' was the brief reply.

The parsonage was set above the church, and my companion suggested that we should lead the horses over the rough path that ran beside it.

'It's not too steep for you, Miss Meredith, is it?' he asked. It was indeed steep, but the climb was exhilarating. At the summit I paused to get my breath.

We were on the fringe of the moors; the dry stone walls ended, and above and beyond, as far as I could see, stretched a great billowing expanse of rugged earth, muted greens and browns, colour melting into colour, under the enormous sky.

Hills rolled along in the distance, great craggy heights towered up, while on the near slopes grey sheep grazed impassively. Cloud shadows danced across the earth, and two birds swooped overhead, crying mournfully.

'Curlews,' said Alec Dewbrey softly. 'They say there are still eagles living on those rocks in the distance.'

For several minutes we stood looking. The wildness and grandeur of the scenery, the solitude of those far hills, and the vastness of the sky made me feel incredibly small and insignificant.

'It must be cruel here in winter,' I murmured.

'Cruel to animal and human alike. But when the spring comes, and the streams gush with melted snow, the wild creatures who have survived run and fly in the sunshine.'

Nevertheless, as we turned and made the descent back into the village, I knew that although he had not said so, lambs and sheep must perish every winter out on those bleak wastes, and beneath the rocks and bracken countless tiny skeletons must lie.

A few days later it became extremely hot again, and I decided to go on the river by myself one afternoon. I got the boat out without any trouble; it creaked satisfyingly as I pulled away from the landing stage. Downstream on the opposite side, I could see the tender mauve shadow of bluebells under the trees.

I was wearing a white muslin dress, sprigged with tiny lilac flowers.

I always wore my hair in ringlets now, a style which Mama disapproved of as being 'frivolous'. As I rowed round the curve of the river, I saw a figure lounging carelessly on the opposite side of the bank. I felt myself blushing — even before I was close enough to recognise his features, I knew that it was Hugh Stacey. As I drew level he stood up, and bowed quite formally.

'Good day, Miss Meredith.'

Seen alone, on the banks of the river, with Swalewell Keep in the background, he looked a mere boy, and strangely lonely, withal.

'Good day, sir,' I replied.

'Do stop and talk a moment, Miss Meredith. Please do.'

How could I resist such an invitation? I steered the boat towards the bank. His fair hair glinted in the sunshine; he smiled enchantingly. After helping me out of the boat, he tied it to an overhanging branch.

'There is a nice patch of grass here, Miss Meredith, and you may sit on this newspaper and talk. I have been staring at the river so long that I thought I was seeing a mirage when you appeared. It's a great comfort to know that you are real.' I laughed gaily; it seemed a bit unreal to me, too. I sat down on the proffered newspaper, with Hugh Stacey beside me.

'How are you enjoying your stay at Ditchford Hall?'

'I am enjoying it very much, thank you,' I answered demurely. It could hardly be called a 'stay', but at that stage I did not feel inclined to explain my position to him. He did not pursue this; instead, he remarked on how competently I rowed.

'I had to do some coaxing before I was allowed to take the boat out myself.'

'I'm glad you coaxed successfully, then.'

The blue eyes gazed into mine

admiringly. Embarrassment and sheer delight struggled within me.

'I'm free most afternoons,' I said. 'I ride a little, or walk in the grounds. I decided it was an ideal day for the river today, though.'

'It's a lazy day,' said Mr. Stacey. 'We decided to be very lazy today.'

'We?' I asked hesitantly.

'My companion, Dryden,' he explained, idly pulling at a tuft of grass. 'He's gone back to the house for something.' He sat smiling at me.

'I'm afraid I can't stay very long,' I said. I could see Mr. Dryden approaching us from the direction of the Keep, although he was still a good way off. For some reason I felt reluctant to stay if he joined us.

'I have an idea, then, Miss Meredith. Come again tomorrow, as soon as you can. I'll bring some lemonade, and we can have a long conversation. How would you like that?'

'Thank you, Mr. Stacey. That would be delightful.'

I saw the surprise on Mr. Dryden's face as he drew close enough to recognise me. He bowed politely, and smiled, and yet I sensed that he no more approved of my being there than Mrs. Dewbrey or Mama would.

Mr. Stacey began telling me about his collection of butterflies. I did not care for this as a hobby.

'They are such pretty things, fluttering about,' I said. 'Surely it is wrong to catch them, just to add to a collection.'

'But my dear Miss Meredith, their lives are so brief in any case.' He nibbled at a blade of grass as he spoke. 'Shortening them for a few hours to look at their beauty for ever — is it wrong?'

'I think so,' I said, but rather doubtfully, because with those vivid blue eyes looking into mine, it was hard to feel strongly about the fate of a few butterflies.

'Then I must catch no more,' said Hugh, turning towards Mr. Dryden, whose only comment was a smile and a shrug.

I found Mr. Stacey's half serious, half bantering manner delightful. Before I left he shook hands, holding my hand just a little longer than was necessary. Then he carefully assisted me into the boat, untied the mooring, and pushed it away from the bank.

'Until tomorrow,' he said, waving. 'Or if it rains, the next sunny day.'

I smiled and nodded, turning the boat around. Both the men watched me from the bank, until they were cut off by the curve of the river. The sun was hot on my face; how foolish of me not to have worn a bonnet! Freckles could hardly be considered attractive, and that was what I wanted Mr. Stacey to think me.

I smiled, remembering his easy charm. Then I turned and glanced upstream, and saw Dan Tulloch and Keeper standing near the boathouse. Faint annoyance stirred in me.

'I'm perfectly all right,' I called out reassuringly, as I drew close. 'I haven't been far — nowhere near that clump of bushes.'

'I wasn't bothered, miss. I just happened to be passing this way.'

I didn't believe that. However, I alighted from the boat unaided, and moored it with Dan Tulloch watching. Then I gave him a quick smile, and walked away from the river side. I had shown him that I was quite capable of handling the boat, and bringing it back safely. My spirits rose; I could hardly stop myself from singing aloud. It was a wonderful, wonderful day!

Mr. Stacey's smile, his elegance, the way he looked at me . . . Georgina would be green with envy!

At tea time I poured the tea, and handed it to Mrs. Dewbrey. 'You are improving greatly with your riding,' she said. She had watched me that morning. 'When you get really proficient you must have a better horse than Pansy. She is good to learn on, but that is not enough.'

As I sat there I wondered just how eccentric Mrs. Dewbrey was. She evidently had plans concerning my riding.

'How well Miss Meredith looks,' observed Mr. Dewbrey at dinner. 'I think country life in Yorkshire is suiting her very well. Don't you agree, Aunt Caroline?'

I kept my eyes modestly fixed on my plate. We were having baked sturgeon, lobster cutlets and salad.

'She is fond of the outdoors — so was I at her age. She tells me she has spent the afternoon writing letters and walking in the grounds. But you must take care, my dear, or the sun will ruin your complexion.'

I felt uncomfortably guilty.

'Dear Aunt, it would take a hotter climate than ours to do that,' said Mr. Dewbrey. 'Besides, there is always plenty of shade under the trees.'

'If the weather stays like this we will do some sketching in the walled garden,' went on his aunt. 'Did you say Mr. Addy and his wife were dining with us this week, Alec?'

I said little, while the other two discussed the everyday events of the neighbourhood.

As soon as I awoke the next morning, I rushed to the window and drew the curtains to one side. It was fine! When Alice arrived with my hot water I felt like throwing my arms around her.

That morning we walked slowly down to the walled garden. It was very pleasant there, with hardly a breath of wind stirring. Stainthorpe, the footman who acted as Mr. Dewbrey's valet — the 'young nowt', as Mrs. Draycott had called him — brought out easels, pencils and paint. We were soon busy, and I perceived that Mrs. Dewbrey worked well and rapidly, even though she herself admitted that she soon tired these days. She seemed pleased with my artistic ability, which I found gratifying. As we painted she talked about the late Mr. Dewbrey, and how they had passed their days at Ditchford Hall. What she did not talk about was her first marriage, or of the dark-haired son whose fate was doubtless still whispered about below stairs.

It was with joyful anticipation that I rowed the boat downstream at last; I was not too pleased at what I saw, though, when I rounded the curve of the river. Sure enough, Mr. Stacey was there, but so was Mr. Dryden. Hugh Stacey greeted me with open pleasure, helped me out, and attended to the boat.

Mr. Dryden, after a polite 'Good day' to me, stood watching us both thoughtfully, his hand resting lightly on his blackthorn walking stick. He must have realised his presence was not required, however, as he announced that he was going into the wood for a stroll.

'I shan't be long,' he added. I watched his sturdy, well-knit frame walk away.

We sat down on the river bank.

'Will your stay at Ditchford Hall be a long one?' asked Hugh. I hesitated before replying.

'I am here as Mrs. Dewbrey's

companion,' I said at last. 'My duties are very light indeed; very pleasant. In the mornings I draw and paint, or walk, or ride. My afternoons are my own, and in the evenings I read to her, or play the piano — or perhaps we play cards.'

'I see,' said Hugh Stacey slowly. 'And you are content, Miss Meredith. Perhaps you have held a similar position before, and found it less pleasant . . . '

'No, I have not,' I said, a little sharply. 'My father is a clergyman, and I have always lived at home. Mrs. Dewbrey particularly requested my services. She knew my parents years ago when my father was a curate of the parish. If I left Ditchford Hall I should not go elsewhere.'

I did not wish him to think that I was bound to earn my bread. Suddenly he picked up my hand, and pressed it to his lips.

'You are lovely — Miss Meredith — Deborah,' he said quietly. I did not withdraw my hand. Overhead I could hear the subdued twitter of birds; for a moment everything seemed to be poised, waiting.

Then, slowly, he drew me into his arms, and his lips met mine, tenderly, gently, almost with a sigh. That first kiss from Hugh Stacey was more like a farewell than anything; the moment trembled, and was gone; the birds still twittered overhead, and yet I felt that nothing would be the same again.

A young and handsome man admired me. Moreover, he was a gentleman who lived in a great house, wore beautiful clothes, and was gallant and charming.

'I suppose you are angry now,' he said with a sigh. 'You cannot imagine how sweet you look, though.'

'No, I'm not angry,' I said, keeping my eyes modestly downcast. 'I have had no dealings with gentlemen before, so I do not know whether I should be.'

He looked at me quizzically, and burst out laughing.

'I beg you — please don't, Miss — er — Deborah. I may call you Deborah, mayn't I?'

'Debbie,' I said. 'Please do.'

Again Hugh held me and kissed me, this time a long, lingering embrace.

'I've brought some lemonade,' he said, some time later, 'and some patties — if you want any. Let me see what's in the basket.'

He produced lemonade, and some glasses. I was very glad of the refreshment, being thirsty, and as I had been too excited to eat much at luncheon, I ate one of the excellent mutton patties. I had never experienced such happiness in my life as I did on that lovely spring afternoon with Hugh Stacey.

'There is no reason why we should not meet every afternoon,' he said.

'No reason at all,' I echoed, but a little uncertainly.

I should have to keep these meetings secret. Mrs. Dewbrey would not approve of them, and neither would her nephew. For a brief moment I thought of Alec Dewbrey, and the displeasure on his face when Hugh Stacey had greeted me after the service at Swalewell church.

I longed to ask Hugh why the two families were not on friendly terms, but I felt I did not know him well enough to ask questions like that yet.

'You're suddenly very serious, Debbie,' he said, biting into a mutton pattie. 'You don't regret coming here, I hope?'

'Indeed no,' I said hastily. 'I was just considering . . . I will come as often as possible, but I can't promise to be here every day. Perhaps you can't promise that, either.'

'I can nearly promise to be here every afternoon — if it is suitable weather, of course. We wouldn't expect to meet in the rain. I have no plans for the summer at all. If at any time I couldn't come, I would try to leave a message for you under that stone.' He indicated a large stone on the bank.

Just then Mr. Dryden appeared, and walked towards us from the woods. I found myself hoping that he would not make a third party at our meetings. It would be most unlikely; no doubt he would be told discreetly when he was not required.

'We've left some lemonade, and one or two morsels for you to eat,' said Hugh, when he reached us.

'Many thanks,' said Mr. Dryden, a faint twinkle in his eyes. 'I'm much obliged, Mr. Hugh.'

Although Hugh called him 'Dryden' and he addressed him as 'Mr. Hugh' there was nothing subservient about his manner towards Hugh Stacey.

He sat down and drank some lemonade. I felt slightly uneasy; I wondered if he guessed that Hugh had kissed me in his absence.

'I shall have to go shortly,' I said, glancing at my watch.

I had to take the boat up the river, and then walk back to the house and get ready for tea with Mrs. Dewbrey.

'As you wish,' said Hugh. 'It's a warm day, and I should not like you to tire yourself out rowing too fast.'

A few minutes later I stepped into the boat; he unmoored it, and I was once again rowing back to the boathouse.

The two men waved from the bank, and then the Beck curved, and cut them off from view.

8

'We are having Mrs. Campion and her daughter Penelope to dine with us tonight,' said Mrs. Dewbrey at tea time. 'When Colonel Campion was alive — and my late husband, Mr. Dewbrey, they were great friends. Mrs. Campion was widowed about three years ago. Penelope is her only child — she is much admired.'

She sat looking thoughtful, and I wondered if Alec Dewbrey was counted among her admirers. I made sure to look my best that evening, and when I saw Penelope Campion looking lovely in a cream coloured gown, I was glad I was wearing a new dress of green taffeta.

A Mr. and Mrs. Sheard, local mill owners, had been invited, but having both developed bad colds they were obliged to decline the invitation. Mrs.

Dewbrey remarked to me before dinner that it seemed rather hard on Alec, being the only gentleman present.

'Puree of wood pigeons — delicious,' murmured Mrs Campion at the dinner table. Although the wine-coloured gown she was wearing was slightly too tight for her thickening figure, she was still a handsome woman. I imagined that like her daughter, she too had been much admired in her day.

Mr. Dewbrey could have spanned Miss Campion's waist with his hands; I was amazed that anyone so tightly laced contrived to eat at all, but she appeared to have a healthy appetite.

'You must ride over one morning, Alec,' she said gaily. 'We are going to give a garden party — like we used to do before Papa was ill.'

'It will mean a lot of work,' put in her mother. 'But we used to give them when Colonel Campion was alive — he did so many things

— nothing was too much trouble.'

'Nobody worked harder,' agreed Mr. Dewbrey.

'You will come along and give it some support, won't you?' asked Miss Campion, her blue eyes beseeching, looking at him.

'Decidedly.'

He smiled indulgently in her direction. Then his glance turned on me.

'I'm sure you would be pleased to take a stall — selling embroidery or something, Miss Meredith.'

'I should be delighted to be of service,' I said. Mrs. Dewbrey looked pleased and interested; she seemed to be looking forward to the proposed garden party.

'I'll probably ride over one morning with Miss Meredith,' said Mr. Dewbrey. 'She has seen little of life outside Ditchford Hall up to now.'

I was rather surprised at this suggestion — I saw surprise on Miss Campion's face, too, although she swiftly hid it.

'That would be a charming idea,' she said smoothly.

After dinner I went into the lovely rose drawing-room with Mrs. Dewbrey and the two other ladies. Mr. Dewbrey remained in the dining-room, smoking a cigar. He said he would follow us in a very short time.

'I think a little music would be very acceptable,' said Mrs. Dewbrey. 'You have not yet played on this piano, Miss Meredith. It has a delightful tone.'

'If the ladies would like it . . . ' I murmured, looking at the ebony grand piano.

'Do play, Miss Meredith,' said Mrs. Campion. 'Penelope, although she has other talents, has never been musically inclined.'

'Miss Meredith sings, too,' added Mrs. Dewbrey.

I felt quite embarrassed. My employer seemed determined to praise me in front of her friends.

I sat down at the piano, and ran my fingers lightly across the keys. For a while I played from the music which was already out. Then, out of the blue, the melody of an old love song came into my mind. Georgina and I had often played it.

'Oh, when can I tell of my own true love? So swift he has taken my heart — and still I must listen with silent lips, denying the beat of my heart . . . '

I began to play the opening bars. Silence fell in the drawing-room, and I knew that Mrs. Dewbrey wanted me to sing. And partly as a duty, and partly because I wanted to, I sang the love song, hauntingly beautiful.

The touch of Hugh Stacey's lips so fresh in my memory gave an added meaning to the tender, poignant words. I forgot the presence of the three ladies, and sang straight from my heart. When I had finished there was a quiet 'Bravo' from behind me, and I turned, startled, to find Mr. Dewbrey had entered the room unobtrusively, and was standing listening.

'You sang that delightfully, Miss

Meredith,' he went on. 'Don't you agree, ladies?'

'Delightfully,' echoed his aunt and Mrs. Campion. Her daughter said nothing, she merely smiled. I sensed hostility beneath the smile, though. Mr. Dewbrey had praised my singing, and she was displeased.

'Do sing something else,' he said. 'Or have we a duet? We could play together.'

He stood looking through the sheets of music. Mrs. Dewbrey looked pleased, while I sat feeling rather nervous at the idea of playing with him.

After a few minutes he selected a piece, saying that he didn't play as often as he should. We sat down together at the piano, and I thought how different his presence was from Georgina's, who was the last person to play a duet with me.

He played extremely well, and yet, to my surprise I felt an ease and confidence which I had not anticipated. My nervousness left me, and I was carried away by the music; the tone of the piano was beautiful, and we played that duet as well as if we had practised it many times.

The others applauded warmly when we had finished, and I felt a glow of achievement. Surely I was performing my duties as a companion more than adequately. Miss Campion evidently thought so too, but not in the same way. Although she smiled, and clapped politely, I sensed that she was feeling displeasure.

'Thank you, Miss Meredith, I enjoyed playing with you,' said Alec Dewbrey. 'Now, pray sing something else, and I will accompany you.'

And that was how we spent the evening, playing and singing, to the delight of Mrs. Dewbrey, and the chagrin of Miss Campion.

Sleep came late to me that night. The events of the day had been too exciting; Hugh Stacey had kissed and admired me, and Mr. Dewbrey had complimented me on my singing, and helped me to entertain the company. Indeed, both he and his aunt had treated me not like a companion in front of their guests, but as an equal.

The following day was fine and warm again, and with a pleasant feeling of anticipation I went down to the boathouse in the afternoon. To my disappointment, though, when I turned the bend in the river, and glanced round, I could see no sign of Hugh.

I drew into the side of the bank at our usual meeting place, and moored the boat carefully on the over-hanging branch. If I lost the boat I would truly be in a plight.

I glanced round nervously before looking under the stone. Sure enough, there was a note for me. I pulled out a piece of expensive but crumpled note-paper.

'I am so sorry, I shall not be able to see you today,' ran the scrawled message. 'Come again — later in the week, perhaps'. It bore the initials H.S.

I screwed the note up in my hand, not sure how to take this rather curt missive. Certainly I was not going to pursue any young man who treated me casually. I looked across at Swalewell Keep, grey and mysterious, surrounded by trees. The green foliage of spring softened the outlook now, but how grim it must appear in winter — how the wind must howl along those stark battlements!

I turned and repressed a little scream of horror at what I saw. I had almost trodden on the horribly mutilated body of a squirrel; some larger animal had caught it and subjected it to frightful torture before killing it. Suddenly I felt sick, and wanted to leave the place as soon as possible. I stepped into the boat, untied it, and rowed back upstream as quickly as I could.

Back in my luxurious bedroom I read through the latest letter from home, and wondered if I was going to be happy at Ditchford Hall after all. I felt unusually tired. I managed to unhook my muslin gown unaided, and slipping it off, I unlaced myself and lay on the bed.

With closed eyes I listened to the twitter of the birds through the open window.

Everything took on a dreamlike quality, even rowing on Swalewell Beck — even the message under the stone, and the mutilated corpse of the squirrel.

The next thing I knew someone was knocking on the bedroom door.

'Come in,' I cried sleepily. Incredible; I had fallen asleep in the middle of the afternoon!

'It's me, miss.' Alice appeared, relief showing on her face. 'It's past tea time, and the mistress has been in a state, wondering where you were. Mr. Alec's been out most of the day, so she couldn't ask him if he'd seen you. I thought you'd 'appen just be in your bedroom — and so you are. Are you feeling well, miss?'

'Yes, I just fell asleep, or I would certainly have joined Mrs. Dewbrey in her sitting-room. Tell her I'll be along very shortly.'

She nodded, and left the room.

Failing my prompt appearance at tea, my employer had raised a hue and cry. It was vexing in a way, and yet, it was flattering, too.

'My dear, I am pleased you are all right,' was her greeting as soon as she saw me. 'Have you been in your room all the time?'

As Mrs. Dewbrey appeared to dislike any mention of Swalewell Beck I said I had been out for a walk, and I supposed the sun had tired me.

'You should have gone for a ride on Pansy,' she said. 'I am coming to see how you are getting on with your riding. I want to see Daisy's foal again, too. Misty — that was the name you gave him, wasn't it?'

'Yes. He is lovely,' I said. 'Gentle and affectionate too, just like Daisy.'

'Yes . . . you know, Miss Meredith, Alec's horse worries me. He would buy that Sorrel, and there was no need.'

I heartily agreed with her. The mere thought of ever riding Sorrel struck fear into me. Not that there was any likelihood; only John Stubbs and Alec Dewbrey dare get at close quarters with the spirited creature.

There was a bark at the door, and I opened it to let Mr. Dewbrey's mastiff, Horatio, in. He was limping slightly.

'Let me see your paw, Horatio,' said Mrs. Dewbrey. 'He got a thorn in, and Alec thought he had better keep to the house today,' she explained. 'He's absolutely wretched, poor creature. We'll give him a few morsels from the table to cheer him up.' I patted his head, and gave him a biscuit.

'I'm surprised you don't have a dog of your own,' I said. An unhappy expression crossed Mrs. Dewbrey's face.

'I did,' she said. 'I had a dear, lively little terrier for several years. In those days I was more active, and we would walk in the grounds together. One day he left me, never to return.'

'You mean — he got lost?' I gently scratched Horatio's ear.

'He was missing for several days. Tulloch and Tresset and Stubbs searched the place for him, but to no avail. Eventually his body was seen in Swalewell Beck — below the weir.'

'Poor little thing,' I said slowly.

'Alec is going to London next week,' she said, changing the subject altogether.

'That is why he has been so busy lately. A distant cousin of his is ill, and he has asked Alec to go and put his affairs in order — quite a task, by all accounts.'

'You will miss Mr. Dewbrey,' I said. 'But the whole place is so well organised that I am sure it will run as usual. If there is anything I can do to help out during his absence . . . '

Mrs. Dewbrey shook her head, smiling. There was a look in her eyes which I could not interpret at all.

'I expect you will miss him too,

particularly around the stables in the mornings.'

'I? Oh, yes, to be sure,' I said hurriedly. The truth of the matter was that I had been thinking Alec Dewbrey's absence would mean still more freedom for me. But would it? If she missed him badly, Mrs. Dewbrey might make more demands on my time than usual. I sipped my tea, thinking it over.

Dr. Denton, the local doctor, came to dinner that night. He was not accompanied by his wife, as she was away on a visit.

He was about fifty, cheerful, sandy-haired, and heavily moustached. He and Mr. Dewbrey remained talking in the dining-room long after Mrs. Dewbrey and I had left it.

'Dr. Denton has been my doctor for a number of years,' she told me. 'We look upon him as a friend of the family. I suppose you think we lead a quiet life here.'

'I have always led a quiet life, I

suppose, so it does not seem so to me,' I assured her.

'I don't entertain much these days. Alec has his circle of friends, but he is a self sufficient sort of man. He could lead a much gayer life than he does, but the truth is he loves country life. He will be missing Ditchford Hall before he's been in London twenty-four hours.'

I realised that she would certainly miss him. Later, Dr. Denton and Mr. Dewbrey joined us, and we spent the evening playing cards. And so the day ended; the day to which I had looked forward so much. The following day the weather broke, and it was wet for the rest of the week.

I played and sang for Mrs. Dewbrey, read to her, painted and did embroidery. But not without a tiny sadness in my heart.

9

By Sunday it was fine again, and I attended morning service with Mrs. Dewbrey. Her nephew had left for London the day before, so we were unaccompanied. I felt myself flushing when Hugh Stacey, the elderly gentleman (whom he had told me was his uncle) and Mr. Dryden took their places in their accustomed pew.

During the service, although I tried not to, I glanced across in Hugh's direction. I caught his eye, and knew that he was still interested in me.

I thought of Alec Dewbrey, embracing his aunt before he left for London, and telling us to take care of each other. He was a baffling sort of man. Sometimes he was remote, abstracted, busy with the affairs of the estate; sometimes he was arrogant and masterful. And yet again, he could be perfectly charming, as on that evening when he sat and played a duet with me.

I wondered if Miss Campion was thinking about him as she sat demurely beside her mother. When we left after the service, I caught Hugh Stacey's eye again, and saw the admiration in his quick glance.

When Mrs. Dewbrey retired to her room after luncheon, I changed into a more suitable dress, and walked down to the boathouse. It was deserted; there was no sign of Dan Tulloch and Keeper. I rowed downstream, and I *knew*, before I looked round, that Hugh Stacey would be on the bank. He was sitting alone, staring across the water, as I came round the curve of the Beck.

'I'm so glad you've come,' he said, as soon as I was within earshot. He tied up the boat, and helped me out. His hands clasped mine, and did not let go.

'I'm so sorry I was unable to come to our last appointment.'

He turned up my face and kissed me, a slow, lingering kiss. When at last he released me I felt guilty, but it had been worth it.

He sat down on the grass, with me on his knee. We talked in whispers, or low voices. I don't know why, except that everything seemed private and precious between us.

'I thought you would come. I haven't brought any lemonade though.'

'It's of no consequence. It's not as though I can stay long — I have to be back to take tea with Mrs. Dewbrey.'

'I see you found my message under the stone.'

'Yes, I found your message.'

Suddenly I thought of the dismembered corpse of the squirrel, and involuntarily glanced towards where it had been. It had gone. Hugh pressed his lips to mine again.

'I've missed you, Debbie.'

'I've missed you, too. Why were you unable to meet me that day?'

'I developed a bad headache, due, no doubt, to riding hatless in the sun. It was most regrettable, but forgive me,

Debbie. Have you thought of me at all?'

'Constantly . . . '

We sat there, kissing and whispering, and sometimes not saying anything for minutes at a time. While we were thus engaged, I saw Mr. Dryden emerge from the woods.

'Here comes Mr. Dryden,' I said, trying to keep the annoyance out of my voice. He seemed to practically live in Hugh's pocket. Surely if Hugh hoped to see me in the afternoons he would drop a hint for the other man to keep away.

They seemed very close, though; it was odd considering there was a difference of several years in their ages.

'Has Mr. Dryden been with you for a long time?' I asked.

'Ever since I was ten. He was my tutor, and a very good one.'

'But you don't need a tutor now.'

'No. But he's such a capital fellow to have around the place — it wouldn't be the same without him.'

I sat thinking about his remark as Mr. Dryden approached us.

'Good day, Miss Meredith,' he said quietly, sitting down in the grass beside Hugh. I had slipped off Hugh's knee on first sighting his companion; I was sitting demurely enough, but I had a feeling that my face was flushed, and my hair a little ruffled.

Did it matter, though, with Mr. Dryden?

We talked about general affairs for a few minutes, and then, almost by mutual agreement, Hugh and I stood up, and he unmoored the boat for me. They both waved to me from the bank.

I'm coming tomorrow, I thought. Tomorrow and tomorrow and tomorrow . . .

That afternoon Mrs. Dewbrey seemed in good spirits as I poured the tea.

'Mrs. Campion has invited us to Clovelly Manor for dinner,' she informed me. 'It is not a big dinner party — we are the only guests.'

'It should be a very pleasant evening,' I said, although I felt sure I had only been included in the invitation out of deference to Mrs. Dewbrey.

Later, I took meticulous care in dressing. In a blue silk gown, provided by my eccentric but generous employer, I hoped I would not look too drab beside Miss Campion.

I had a longing for Hugh Stacey to see me thus. When Alice had finished doing my hair I twirled around, and my skirts swished enchantingly. I felt miserable and madly happy all at once.

John Stubbs drove us through the village, and some way beyond. It was a light, bright evening; the lambs were well grown now, and made a pretty picture grazing in the meadows with their mothers. Clovelly Manor, although large, was not a great rambling place like Ditchford Hall. Unlike most dwelling places in the district, it was built of brick, not stone. My first impression was that it looked inviting, and indeed, the house had a charm all its own.

Colonel Campion had travelled extensively, and lived abroad for many years.

The house was full of the treasures he had collected. The drawing-room contained carved stools, Chinese scrolls, and a chest; there was a very beautiful screen, and numerous vases, figurines, and ivory animals.

Both ladies greeted us kindly, and yet I still sensed this curious hostility behind Miss Campion's polite smile.

The dinner was very good, served by an Indian servant who had obviously been with the family for years.

'Now what is this dish called?' enquired Mrs. Dewbrey. 'I've had it when I've dined here before.'

'Pooloot,' said Mrs. Campion. 'Penelope and I both love it.'

'So do I. It's delectable — the flavour of ginger with lemons — and the chicken so delicious. I would love Mrs. Tukes to try making this dish, but I don't think she could do it like your — what is his name?'

'Ram Singh,' smiled our hostess. 'He likes to make these special dishes *and* serve at table, which he manages very well if the dinner party is small.'

He was indeed efficient. He moved silently, resplendent in his high buttoned white satin tunic. Although well past his youth he was erect and handsome. Miss Campion caught me looking at him — after all, I had never been waited on by an Indian before — and smiled mischievously.

'He can foretell the future, too,' she said. 'Only he won't do it for me — but I know he can! Our maid, Jennie, told me. I've no doubt he could tell you all sorts of things, Miss Meredith . . . '

I felt my colour rise under her mocking gaze.

'Really, Penelope,' said her mother, in an indulgently chiding voice, 'how you do run on. Pray don't talk such nonsense.'

'It's not nonsense, it's quite true,' she persisted. 'He knows, but he won't always tell what he knows. Do tell Miss Meredith what the future holds for her, Ram Singh.'

A silence fell across the table as Ram

Singh deftly served the sweet. His eyes met mine for a moment. I could feel my cheeks flaming now — I felt that nothing was secret from that dark, inscrutable gaze. He straightened up.

'You have made a great change,' he said softly. 'There are greater changes ahead for you . . . I must warn the memsahib against people who would work evil. The memsahib is looking for happiness — it will not come in the way she thinks. There will be great sadness first . . . great sadness . . . I can tell no more now.'

He bowed and withdrew, leaving me shaken and disturbed. I did not know what strange power this man possessed, but I saw knowledge in his dark eyes, knowledge of some nameless evil; knowledge of things past and present, and things which must remain forever secret. A cold shiver ran through me.

'Don't look so alarmed, Miss Meredith,' said Mrs. Campion, smiling reassuringly. 'Ram Singh was merely saying something to oblige Penelope. Dismiss it from your mind, my dear. She is full of strange fancies . . . '

'Be warned,' interrupted her daughter, a disarming smile on her lovely face. 'Happiness will not come in the way you think.'

'Happiness, if it comes at all, never does come in the way we think,' put in Mrs. Dewbrey, with a rather sad smile. 'One does better to live from day to day — don't you agree, Mrs. Campion?'

'Indeed I do. I might have buried all my happiness with my husband — and so might you — but life must go on. Of course, all young people imagine that love is happiness, and happiness is love.'

'Happiness . . . ' murmured her daughter. Her blue eyes took on a softer, more appealing look, and a tender smile curved her pouting red lips. For a moment she sat without speaking; but I well knew what she was thinking. Happiness for her meant only one thing; to be Alec Dewbrey's wife.

Although it was Sunday we played whist in the charming drawing-room for the rest of the evening. It was plain that Mrs. Dewbrey desired her friends to accept me as a social equal, and she was sufficiently well esteemed by others to have her wishes respected, outwardly at all events.

Inevitably, the conversation turned to Mr. Dewbrey.

'I expect him to be in London for about a month,' said his aunt, frowning with concentration as she surveyed her hand of cards. 'He went in the course of duty — not pleasure. He cares nothing for London.'

'So very odd,' murmured Miss Campion. 'Perhaps he does not have the society of agreeable people when he is there.'

'I hardly think that is the reason. After all, he lived just outside London for years when he was young — no, I think he is a countryman at heart, if not by birth.'

'I freely admit I adore London,' said Miss Campion. 'What do you say, Miss Meredith?'

'There is certainly a great deal to see and do,' I said, a reply which did not commit me. 'To live there all the time, though — no, I do not think I should care for that, particularly in summer.'

Mrs. Dewbrey nodded her head approvingly. Mrs. Campion stole a rather worried glance at her daughter. I wondered if she hoped the girl would make a match of it with Alec Dewbrey, and whether she and his aunt had discussed the possibility between them.

Although Clovelly Manor was not such a large establishment as Ditchford Hall, nevertheless the Campions lived in style. She would not be a penniless bride.

I wondered what Alec Dewbrey's feelings were towards her. Still thinking about this, I put down the King of Hearts, and Miss Campion immediately trumped it with an ace.

'What a surprise from Penelope,' commented Mrs. Campion.

'And the moral of that,' said her daughter, 'is never show your hand unless you are sure you hold the trump card.'

As she said this, I knew that her words were double-edged, and intended for me. For some reason she seemed afraid that I might be a rival for Alec Dewbrey's affections, paid companion though I was.

If she only knew that I was waiting for an opportunity to dream about Hugh Stacey! To imagine rowing down the river again to meet him . . .

'I trust Alec will be back in time to help with the garden party,' said Mrs. Campion. 'We are going ahead with our plans for it.'

'If you like, I'll make some treacle toffee for it,' I said. 'I used to make quantities for church bazaars, and things like that.'

'What a splendid idea!' exclaimed Mrs. Campion. 'You could have a stall and sell it, Miss Meredith.'

'With pleasure,' I replied.

Mrs. Dewbrey looked pleased. 'I'm sure Mrs. Tukes will let you have charge of the kitchen for that occasion.'

Later, as John Stubbs drove us back, I decided it had been an interesting evening. Despite the disadvantages of my position, I felt I had stood up well to Miss Campion's rather sly baiting. But that strange manservant, Ram Singh, what had he meant?

* * *

The next afternoon I rowed down Swalewell Beck again, and saw Hugh waiting for me on the bank.

'I'm so glad you could come, Debbie,' he greeted me.

As soon as he had moored the boat I felt his arms around me, so tightly that the breath seemed to be squeezed out of me for a moment. I pushed away, and he released me, smiling down at me.

'You should always wear pink,' he said softly. 'I have never seen anyone look so pretty. Come on, sit down with me, further back from the Beck.'

Hand in hand we moved away from the bank, to a patch well shaded by trees.

'I've been looking forward to this ever since you left me yesterday,' he said.

'So have I.'

'What have you been doing since I last saw you?'

'Last night we dined at the Campions. Do you know them?'

After a slight pause he said that Colonel Campion used to visit his uncle. We were sitting side by side on his jacket, which he had removed and laid on the grass. He plucked a piece of grass and nibbled it nervously, which I thought a curious habit for a well-bred gentleman.

'Then you will know Miss Campion — Penelope?' I persisted.

There was a brooding, bitter expression on his face. For a moment he stared straight ahead.

'Have you no friends in the neighbourhood?' I asked.

'I don't bother with people very much,' he said, after some hesitation. 'I have Dryden.'

There was something baffling about Hugh Stacey and the way he lived.

'Are you happy, Hugh?' I asked.

Again he did not reply immediately. He rolled over on the grass, and lay on his back, looking at me.

'At this very moment, yes, I am happy, Debbie. Happy because we can sit in the sunshine and kiss, and not care about anything else, just for a while.'

He twisted one of my ringlets round his finger.

'Say you're happy, Debbie,' he whispered.

'Of course I'm happy, being with you.'

'Happier than you have ever been?'

'Happier than I have ever been.'

It was true. He was the living fulfilment of all my romantic dreams. Even as his arms were around me, and his lips pressed to mine I was thinking how envious Georgina would be if she could see me.

'Would you care for a short stroll in the woods?' he asked presently. 'It is so pleasant and shady. We have time.'

He stood up, and drew me slowly to my feet. We walked along under the thick foliage of the trees.

'Do you like trees — and woods?'

'Yes . . . ' I gave a little gasp as a grey squirrel darted out and ran in front of us, and up a tree. I was suddenly reminded of the tiny, mutilated corpse I had seen on the river bank. The clearing ahead was covered with bluebells.

'I'll pick you a posy,' said Hugh. 'Then you can press it between the leaves of a book, and when you are old and grey, you can open it, and remember me.'

'Don't talk such nonsense,' I replied, feeling suddenly depressed.

He stooped and picked a little nosegay, and gave it me. There was a movement behind me, and a cough.

'So we're all going for a walk in the

woods,' came Mr. Dryden's calm, matter-of-fact voice. I turned to see him standing behind us. I had a curious impression that he had been watching from some vantage point, and had followed us at a discreet distance.

'I think it's time I was making my homeward journey,' I said, and Hugh did not demur. We strolled back to where the boat was moored. Dryden lingered in the woods; I supposed this was thoughtfulness on his part, but I felt little gratitude.

Before I stepped into the boat we stood in a long embrace.

'Come tomorrow,' he said. There was scarcely any need for him to say that. I fell to dreaming as I rowed back. If he had only been a Campion instead of a Stacey he would have been welcome at Ditchford Hall. Everything would have been different.

With a sigh I moored the boat, hoping that it would not rain the following day.

Back in the house I changed and

composed myself preparatory to taking tea with Mrs. Dewbrey. The life which I had thought was going to be so boring was proving very different.

'The doctor and his wife are dining with us tonight,' said Mrs. Dewbrey. 'Did I mention it before, Debbie? Sometimes I forget things. His wife is charming — very kind. You have met her coming out of church . . . '

She had fallen into the habit of gossiping in the pleasantest way about our neighbours, with the exception of the Staceys. She never mentioned them.

After a while she began to talk about her nephew, and how busy he was in London. Then the conversation turned to the garden party.

'Mrs. Campion is holding a ball in the evening after the garden party. Colonel Campion always used to do that. The servants prepare the long gallery, and they hire musicians from Halifield. They usually have a house party at the same time, so the guests who are staying attend the ball, as well as people who live locally.'

I supposed that as I was helping at the garden party, I would also be invited to the ball.

'You've been neglecting your riding lately, Debbie, so that we could paint together. Leave me tomorrow morning and go for a canter. I'll come down to the stables with you though, and see how Misty is going on.'

It occurred to me that evening that Dr. Denton must be Hugh's doctor, too. Apart from anything else, that simple fact endeared him to me. His wife was a sweet, vague woman, whose hair seemed just on the point of falling down. They were a nice couple; indeed, all Mrs. Dewbrey's friends seemed agreeable people.

There was, of course, Penelope Campion's antagonistic attitude towards me — no, that was too strong a word. As usual, my thoughts turned to Hugh Stacey, and I wondered how he passed his time when he was away from me. Although we talked when we were together, I never seemed to find out much about him. I had put his nosegay between the pages of my bible, and before going to bed that night I opened it again. The smell of crushed bluebells filled my nostrils.

10

The next day was even warmer, and I surveyed the blue, cloudless sky with satisfaction as Alice arranged my hair. I was wearing my riding habit, and I felt happy and light-hearted. With surprise and pleasure I greeted Mrs. Dewbrey in the breakfast room. It was the first time she had breakfasted there since I had come to Ditchford Hall.

After breakfast we took a few sugar lumps and walked along to the stables. Daisy's foal, Misty, was growing rapidly; a lovable, leggy little creature, with a soft, nuzzling nose. Mrs. Dewbrey and I fed him the sugar lumps, not forgetting his mother, Daisy.

'Aye, he's bonny, isn't he, madam?' John Stubbs was busy in the stable yard. 'But that villain . . . '

He nodded towards Sorrel's stall.

'Are you riding him in Mr. Dewbrey's absence?'

'I am that, madam. He nearly had me off yesterday, though. He's getting worse, I'm sure of that.'

He laughed as he spoke, but Mrs. Dewbrey did not appear amused. I had gathered from previous conversations that her nephew had taken a fancy to the creature and bought him from an acquaintance some twelve months earlier. The groom saddled Pansy and led her out. I cantered her gently round the yard, while Mrs. Dewbrey watched approvingly.

'She has an excellent seat, don't you think?' she enquired of John Stubbs.

'Excellent, madam. I have never seen any young lady take to it more naturally.'

I smiled with pleasure, and reined in Pansy.

She patted the animal. 'You go for a canter, my dear. I'm just going to stroll along to the walled garden, and sit there for a while.'

I waved to her, and set off at a smart jogtrot. Almost without being conscious of it, I made for the river.

I walked Pansy along the bank as far as we could go, to where the thick hedge marked the boundary line between the Dewbreys' land and that of a tenant farmer, Mr. Kymes.

Pansy stood quietly for a few minutes, and I looked down the river, wondering who lived in the little stone cottage built so close to the water's edge, on the Staceys' side.

And in the afternoon I returned, and rowed downstream as usual. Hugh was there to greet me — alone. If only Dryden would keep away for the next hour or so!

Hugh helped me out of the boat, and swept me into his arms. He held me so close, and kissed me so hard that for a moment I had a sensation of panic — besides, the boat was as yet unmoored.

'The boat!' I cried. 'Tie it up, Hugh, or it will drift.'

He laughingly released me, and tied up the boat, much to my relief.

Then he took me in his arms again. As he kissed me I forgot all about Ditchford Hall and my duties as a companion.

I only knew that I was glad I had met Hugh Stacey, no matter how. We sat holding hands and kissing, not saying very much.

'I shan't be able to row downstream when the summer's over,' I remarked, after a long, sweet silence.

'When the summer is over . . . no, Debbie, please don't talk like that. Don't think of the future.'

'But I must — everybody must, Hugh.'

A brightly coloured butterfly sank with trembling wings onto a patch of clover beside us. We both watched it, then Hugh reached out with a swift movement, and enclosed it in his hand.

He smiled at me.

'How hard it struggles to be free!'

'Let it go,' I said, having no taste at

all for this sort of thing. He slowly uncurled his fingers, and it flew away from danger, leaving a dusting of powder from its wings on his hand. He took out a lawn handkerchief and wiped away the traces of his tiny prisoner. 'A Red Admiral. A common variety, anyway.'

'You promised not to catch any more.'

'Nor have I. I was only teasing you, Debbie. Forgive me.' What was there to forgive? He kissed me with great tenderness.

'Who lives in that little cottage further down the river?' I asked, some time later.

'Why do you ask?'

'Just curiosity, I suppose.'

'An old man named Jonas Wilkins. He's been with the family for years. He was a gamekeeper at one time.'

'Oh,' I said.

He kissed me again, dismissing the matter, and asked me how I had spent the day.

'Mrs. Dewbrey insisted that I should leave her this morning, and go for a ride. I felt a bit reluctant to, because Mr. Dewbrey is in London, and I know she misses him.'

'Ah,' he said, half to himself, 'so Dewbrey is away.'

Just then I saw the familiar figure of Mr. Dryden strolling out of the woods. Irritation rose in me as always at his approach. It could not really be said that we were unchaperoned; Hugh's companion appeared to have taken on the task.

He greeted me politely as always. I forced a tight little smile to my lips, but never had the sight of him been less welcome.

'I must go presently, Hugh,' I said. 'I must be there at tea time.'

'Tomorrow, then,' he murmured, giving my hand a squeeze.

For the next few days we met as arranged. Each day, sooner or later Dryden would appear — I had reached the conclusion that Hugh was too kind to tell him he was not welcome — so, perforce, I had to put on a smile and make the best of it.

When I was not with Hugh I would be dreaming about him, but I was not altogether happy. I was far from worldly-wise, but I had read enough novels to know that gentlemen sometimes dallied with girls of lesser social position. The idea that Hugh could have that attitude towards me was most distasteful, and yet, I was unable to put the thought entirely out of my mind.

Other things worried me too — this cold, silent enmity between the Dewbreys and the Staceys — something never discussed, but always there.

'Your family and Mrs. Dewbrey's — please tell me why they are not friendly,' I said coaxingly one day.

'The Dewbreys!' he said scornfully. 'They're of no account! Do you expect me, a Stacey, to trouble myself thinking about them? Swalewell Keep was first built as a Norman fortress — my ancestor built the church the Dewbreys drive to on Sundays — oh, Debbie, you don't understand!'

His outburst frightened me.

'We had been living here centuries before the Caldecotts came,' he went on. 'It was bad enough — the airs and graces the Caldecotts gave themselves . . . but my God, the Dewbreys!'

He was so roused I heartily wished I had never brought the matter up.

'Do you know Ditchford Hall belonged to the Caldecotts?'

'Yes — the housekeeper told me — in fact Mr. Dewbrey told me first.'

'He has a high opinion of himself,' said Hugh, his voice contemptuous. 'He's of no account — an upstart who goes around acting the squire.'

'Hardly an upstart,' I protested. 'Mr. Dewbrey is — well — er — he is a gentleman.'

Hugh gave a short, derisive laugh. 'Setting himself up,' he muttered. 'They have *their*, family skeletons rattling around — there's a lot of dirty linen *they* wouldn't like to wash in public.'

He then dismissed the subject, and although my curiosity was aroused, I was relieved.

After his outburst against the Dewbreys, though, I felt more uneasy than ever about our secret meetings. It was obvious that his family pride was strong; I would never be more than a passing flirtation in his life. And yet, he waited so eagerly for our meetings . . . it was all so difficult. The truth was that I could not bear the idea of not seeing him. It was so wonderful to know that I would be clasped in his arms every afternoon, that I was free to dream about him most of the day, and write about him in my diary at night.

Mr. Dewbrey was prolonging his stay in London. In view of this, I was scarcely surprised to learn that Miss Campion was travelling to London for a short stay with an aunt, who was then returning to Yorkshire with her.

'No doubt Miss Campion and Mr. Dewbrey will see each other in London then?' I suggested.

'They may.' Mrs. Dewbrey's reply was guarded, and I was left with the feeling that she was not very pleased about something. She changed the subject and said that if I wanted to go for a canter on Pansy that morning, she was well content to sit in the walled garden.

By now I deemed myself a good enough horsewoman to ride out to the village, and turned Pansy's head in the direction of Swalewell.

The countryside round about was becoming less strange to me; I knew the road from Ditchford Hall to the village very well, but on this occasion I had the fancy to do some exploring. Having cantered Pansy round Swalewell, I had an idea I could get back a different way.

I turned down a narrow lane, and saw a bridge spanning Swalewell Beck. I glanced beyond it, and there, further along, was the little grey cottage on the Staceys' side of the river. I could see the weir now; how rough the water was as it dropped like a sheer wall, and rushed along, foaming. I reined in Pansy, and sat for a while, looking. I had a sudden overwhelming urge to ride up to that cottage and have a closer look at it. I urged Pansy forward slowly.

As we approached it I could see that it was indeed dilapidated. Dirty curtains hung forlornly at the windows; the garden, which must have been well kept at one time, was a wilderness of coarse grass and weeds. The paint had long since peeled off from the broken fence, and the whole place had an atmosphere of sadness and decay.

There was no sign of life within. The next moment two horsemen appeared from the other side of the cottage. I was very taken aback to recognise Hugh Stacey and Dryden. Feeling acutely embarrassed I reined in Pansy as they approached me. What would Hugh think? He might not be too pleased to find me there, trespassing on the Stacey land; exploring without permission.

At the same time I was glad my

riding habit was well cut, and became me so well.

'Good day, Debbie,' he called, as soon as we were close enough. Both he and Dryden doffed their hats, and rode up to me.

'I just had a canter into the village,' I explained. 'I thought perhaps I could get back another way.'

'Across the bridge?' enquired Hugh.

'Well, yes. And then I decided to have a look at the weir — and then I thought I would like to see the cottage . . . '

'You're trespassing, young lady,' said Hugh with mock severity. 'You must have seen the notice 'Private Land' as you turned off the footpath.'

'And the land opposite — where the bridge comes out?'

'If you go along that lane, and turn right, you'll come onto Farmer Kymes' place — you can get back that way, if you just follow the Beck.'

'I thought so,' I said, feeling more relaxed.

Hugh seemed pleased to see me. He

looked well in the saddle, mounted on a splendid grey horse. Dryden was riding a Cleveland Bay. He had replaced his hat, and sat without speaking, his face expressionless.

I glanced beyond him at the cottage, and noticed that an old man had come out of it, and was walking up the path to the broken gate. He was wearing a shabby pair of corduroy trousers and a dirty blue shirt. His grey hair was still thick, but long and matted, like his beard. He looked tired and dazed.

'Good day, Wilkins,' called Hugh, who had seen him too.

'Good day — er — Mr. Hugh.'

The old man stood at the gate, looking uncertainly in our direction. Then his eyes became riveted on me. I sat stock still on Pansy, while his gaze searched my face.

For a long minute Hugh, Dryden and I were silent. I do not know why we all three sat thus while this old man inspected me.

Then, suddenly, a cry broke from

him; a hoarse cry of anguish which seemed as though torn from the depth of human sorrow.

'Caldecott!' he cried, pointing at me with a trembling finger. 'Caldecott!'

11

As soon as I opened my eyes I could hear the rain beating against the window. Discontent spread through me. My thoughts went back to the morning earlier in the week when I had met Hugh and Dryden on the Stacey land.

What had that strange old man meant by shouting 'Caldecott!' at me? I had not seen Hugh since; at lunchtime that day heavy clouds had gathered, and darkened the sky. A thunderstorm followed, and the rain came down wand straight, as if it would never stop. This was the fourth day of rain, and I was beginning to despair of the fine weather ever returning. The only thing which made the day bearable was the thought that it would soon be Sunday, and I would at least see Hugh in church.

When Sunday came, it was still raining, but very lightly; I held an umbrella over Mrs. Dewbrey and myself as we walked through the churchyard. From our pew, I glanced swiftly across the aisle, and to my disappointment saw only the figure of Hugh's uncle. Hugh and Dryden were both missing.

On Monday it rained again, but when Tuesday dawned, dull but dry, I made up my mind that I would go down the river if at all possible. The banks of the Beck were squelching wet and muddy; expecting that, I had put on a serviceable costume, and wore boots.

I could feel my heart beating faster as I neared the bend in the river. I glanced round — yes, there was a figure standing on the bank. He was there! But when I drew closer, disappointment and apprehension spread through me. It was not Hugh — it was Dryden.

Hugh must be ill! In spite of a feeling of reluctance to be in Dryden's company by myself, I continued to row towards him.

'Good day, Miss Meredith,' he said,

as I steered the boat in to the bank.

'Good day,' I replied.

'I shan't keep you a moment,' he said gravely, 'I came along to tell you Mr. Hugh is not very well.'

'Not very well! What is wrong with him? A chill?'

'Something of that nature. He will certainly be indoors for the rest of the week.'

'Oh,' I said, somewhat blankly. Was there no letter, no message for me? 'Thank you for troubling to come and tell me,' I added, although I had no doubt Hugh had asked him to.

'It's no trouble — but Miss Meredith, I do advise you in all sincerity not to come down the Beck to see Mr. Hugh any more.'

For a moment I was too astonished to speak — the sheer impertinence of the man! It was bad enough to have him always appearing on the scene when I wanted to be alone with Hugh, but to 'advise' me to keep away — how dare he?

'Indeed,' I said coldly, with all the dignity I could muster, 'may I ask why?'

'No, you may not,' was the reply; my dignity had not impressed him. 'I am asking you, for your own good, to keep away. It is better for both of you if this acquaintanceship is dropped now. I do not want Mr. Hugh upset . . . I do not want anyone upset. Please keep away, Miss Meredith.'

I could feel myself trembling. I was completely taken aback. I was angry too, at his dismissing me as a mere acquaintance.

'You're jealous of me,' I said slowly, my feelings of antagonism rising to the surface. 'You want Hugh all to yourself. That's why you're always somewhere around when we meet. I wonder Hugh permits it . . . '

'I don't wish to listen to your ridiculous accusations. You are very young and very innocent. Now off you go, and I hope not to see you again except in church.'

I could find nothing more to say. In

silence I turned the boat round, and began to row upstream.

As I moored the boat I made up my mind to be patient until Hugh was well again. I would ignore what Dryden had said to me.

As I approached the house, Horatio, Mr. Dewbrey's dog, came bounding across the grass to meet me. We had become great friends during his master's absence, and although I was not in a happy mood, I had to smile as he lolloped towards me with his big tongue hanging out, and his tail wagging.

'Come on, Horatio, we'll go for a stroll around the house,' I said. I allowed him to lead me, and then I realised where he was making for. He wanted to get back into the house through the scullery and kitchen. As I walked with him through the scullery I heard voices from the kitchen.

'I always say it doesn't do to listen to gossip.' That was the voice of the housekeeper, Mrs. Draycott.

'Well, Mrs. Draycott, you know me.

I'm not in the habit of either listening to it or repeating it . . . ' That was the cook, Mrs. Tukes.

'But I was here when she was Mrs. Caldecott, and I can remember things. You mark my words, Mrs. Draycott, there's more in it than meets the eye . . . '

At this point Horatio pushed forward with a loud bark, and I followed him through the scullery and into the great, roomy kitchen.

Mrs. Tukes and Mrs. Draycott were sitting down drinking tea. None of the maids were about. They both flushed up when I appeared with the dog — indeed, so embarrassed did they seem that I guessed I had only heard the tail end of some very confidential matter they had been discussing.

'Why, Miss Meredith!' exclaimed the housekeeper. 'What are you doing down here?'

'I'm sorry, have I given you a start bursting in on you?' I asked. 'I met Horatio in the grounds, and he took me for a very short walk, which ended here.'

'Aye, it would, miss,' said Mrs. Tukes, covering her confusion with a nervous laugh. 'He knows he can usually beg a bone or some titbit from me.'

After a brief conversation, I walked out of the kitchen, leaving Horatio gnawing at a large bone. I went up to my room, and looked through the window. The weight of the rain had beaten the flowers and shrubs down; the heads of the rhododendrons drooped sadly.

I sat down and thought of Hugh not being well, and of what Dryden had said. I thought too of the strange man, Wilkins, who had seemed so disturbed on seeing me near his cottage.

And finally I thought about the conversation down in the kitchen. Had I been there a few minutes earlier, what would I have heard? I had a feeling that I had been mentioned in that private discussion between the cook and the housekeeper; they had both looked so embarrassed and surprised.

I wrote a letter home, and then, to cheer myself up, I changed into a particularly pretty dress of white organdie, and threw a white silk shawl over my shoulders, before going to Mrs. Dewbrey's sitting-room. She was not there; probably she had spent the afternoon resting on her bed.

I picked up my embroidery, intending to do a few stitches, when there was a quick knock at the door, and Alec Dewbrey appeared with Horatio prancing excitedly behind him. I stood up, utterly astonished at seeing him back. Mrs. Dewbrey had said that he would remain in London for another week at least.

'Good day, Miss Meredith,' he said, his eyes running over me searchingly. 'I am pleased to see you looking so well.'

'Thank you, sir,' I replied, recovering my composure. 'We did not expect you today. Shall I ring for tea now? Mrs. Dewbrey should be here presently. Have you been in the house long?'

'About half an hour. I left London this morning. I didn't wish to disturb my aunt, as I know she rests in the afternoon. My cousin appears to be gaining strength, and I took the opportunity of returning, for a while at least.'

His masculine bulk seemed to fill the room, although, judged by Ditchford Hall standards, it was not a large room. Still, it was not a small room, either.

It struck me forcibly that Alec Dewbrey diminished his surroundings, and not merely because he had a good physique. His dark, commanding eyes seemed to be looking right through me. I felt uneasily guilty in his presence.

I rang for tea, but before it arrived Mrs. Dewbrey came in, and greeted her nephew with surprised delight. A few minutes later Ida appeared with the tea, and I busied myself with the tea things, taking little part in the conversation which followed, a good deal of which concerned the Dewbrey family.

'Have you seen Miss Campion in

London?' enquired Mrs. Dewbrey after a while.

He replied that he had. Naturally, I thought. That was her motive in going there.

'I suppose she is having a gay time,' his aunt commented.

'I believe so. No doubt you will hear how much she has enjoyed herself when she returns.'

'Her mother prefers the quiet of the country.'

'Yes. Many people do,' remarked her nephew. He caught my eye, and again the feeling of guilt came over me.

He went on to talk about local affairs, even enquiring after the village cricket team, about which, not surprisingly, neither of us could tell him much. Horatio gazed up at him adoringly — his beloved master had returned. Looking at him sitting there, his hound at his knee, I thought of Hugh's bitter words about him — 'He's of no account . . . an upstart who goes around acting the squire . . . '

'It was bad enough, the airs and graces the Caldecotts gave themselves . . . '

'Caldecott! Caldecott!'

The anguished cry of the old man who lived in the cottage came back to me.

'Miss Meredith is far away.'

'I beg your pardon — did you speak?'

The bantering tone of Alec Dewbrey's voice jerked me back to the present with a start.

'Debbie can be excused for daydreaming a little,' said his aunt. 'We have been discussing family affairs, while she has been pouring tea and handing cakes round.'

'There is no harm in daydreaming — the age of miracles has not yet passed,' said her nephew dryly. After a few minutes, he rose and excused himself, saying that he wanted a word with Dan Tulloch.

'What is going to happen concerning the garden party which the Campions were going to have?' I asked when I was alone with Mrs. Dewbrey.

'I expect it will be held as planned. No doubt Miss Campion will be back soon.'

She sat pensively for several minutes. Would a match between her nephew and her friend's daughter please her? I wondered. A marriage between a man who was . . . what?

Arrogant? Self sufficient? Proud? I found it difficult to judge the qualities which made up Alec Dewbrey — less difficult in the case of Miss Campion. She was attractive, vain and shallow. She was also very spoilt. But if her nephew married this girl, what need would Mrs. Dewbrey have for my services?

Then I thought of Hugh Stacey.

I was sure he was not just flirting with me; there was a great deal more than that to it. Not for the first time I gave myself up to the delicious, impossible dream of a future shared wholly with him. Anyway, the long, golden summer lay ahead of us, and, despite Dryden's warning, I would meet him at the first opportunity.

It would not be that week, of course. But if he attended church the following Sunday, I would know he was well again. Meanwhile, I had much to occupy myself with. I was not surprised to learn that Penelope Campion was returning from London later in the week. On the Sunday Mrs. Dewbrey developed a chill, and was unable to attend church with her nephew and me.

I sat opposite him in the carriage.

'I understand from Stubbs that you are doing very well as a horsewoman,' he said.

'I have been riding most days during your absence. I went into the village one morning on Pansy.'

'Alone?'

'Yes. I took a short cut back to the house through Farmer Kymes' place, down by the Beck.'

A look of displeasure crossed his face.

'I would prefer you not to ride out of

the grounds until you are more experienced — not unaccompanied, anyway.'

I felt quite taken aback at the cool way he had stated his wishes.

'I am extremely sorry, sir,' I said tartly. 'Perhaps you will give me a list of instructions next time you have occasion to leave the house.'

'Yes. It would simplify matters,' he said, ignoring my tone of voice. 'It is scarcely fair to expect a lady my aunt's age to be responsible for your well-being, although she is officially your employer. At eighteen you are not your own mistress, and while you reside at Ditchford Hall you are under my care.' I sat tensely in the carriage, resenting his words and the calm way in which he had uttered them.

I thought of the afternoons I had spent with Hugh. I had little doubt as to what he would think of those. Outside the churchyard, my heart gave a tremendous thud as I saw Hugh with his uncle and Dryden going through the gate. Alec Dewbrey helped me out of the carriage, and his eyes followed my gaze. I had the sense to avert it, but as we went into church I noticed he was frowning slightly.

I knelt beside him, trying to compose myself, although the relief and excitement of seeing Hugh almost made me forget what I was at church for. I wondered if Penelope Campion's thoughts were equally undisciplined as she sat there in her costly blue outfit.

After the service we emerged into the bright sunlight; as usual, the Staceys did not linger in the churchyard. Nevertheless, Hugh passed close to me, and our eyes met. The look in his told me clearly that he would be there the next time I took the boat down the river.

Mrs. Campion and her daughter came up to us, and there was much chatter from Penelope about London, and how she had enjoyed her stay there.

'And your dear aunt — she is not well, then?' interposed Mrs. Campion.

'Just a chill — very slight, but I persuaded her to stay in today. She should be recovered in a couple of days.'

'Tell her she must avoid getting any more chills — we are having the garden party in two weeks' time . . . ' Miss Campion paused. 'You will help us, Alec, won't you?'

Her china-blue eyes gazed up into his dark ones. Her soft, fair hair peeped out from under her elaborate bonnet; her expensively gloved hands fluttered appealingly.

'To be sure I'll help you,' he said, smiling. 'I'll help set up the stalls, and provide sacks for the sack race.'

'And don't forget, Miss Meredith, you promised to make treacle toffee,' said Mrs. Campion.

'I shall be delighted to,' I said. I was bubbling over with happiness — soon I would be in Hugh's arms again.

'I used to be very fond of treacle toffee,' said Alec Dewbrey. 'I never knew you possessed such talent, Miss Meredith.'

His eyes were dancing; I flushed under his amused gaze. What a strange man he was. He could be brusque; arrogant on occasions; at other times he could be light-hearted and charming.

After a few minutes' further conversation, we got into our respective carriages. John Stubbs clicked his tongue at the horses, and I saw Penelope Campion cast a last glance in Alec Dewbrey's direction before we drove away. I sat in silence, thinking about Hugh.

My companion was silent, too.

I wondered what his thoughts were, and if they concerned the fair beauty who was so in love with him. A strange love affair, I thought, and so different from my own.

Then I began to dream about Hugh, while the horses' hooves clip-clopped rhythmically down the country lanes.

The man who had told me I was under his authority sat opposite me, his face impassive.

12

I rowed downstream that afternoon, thinking of Dryden's warning to keep away from Hugh. Suppose Hugh was missing again, and Dryden was there? Suppose . . . but no, I breathed a sigh of relief. Hugh was waiting on the bank.

'Debbie! My darling!'

I was clasped in his arms, my heart beating wildly.

'I've missed you so!' I gasped. 'I wondered what was wrong . . . '

He held me at arm's length. 'But Dryden told you I had a chill?'

I repressed an impulse to repeat to him all that Dryden had said. Perhaps I would some time; at the moment our shared happiness was too sweet.

We stood clasped in each other's arms, on the sodden banks of the swollen river. It was far too damp everywhere to think of sitting down.

‘We’ll go for a walk in the woods,’ said Hugh, drawing my arm through his.

‘When did you first hear you were coming to Ditchford Hall?’ he asked, as we walked along.

‘A few weeks before my eighteenth birthday,’ I said. ‘It was such a surprise, Hugh. I couldn’t understand why a lady I had never met should send for me. But papa had been the curate here years ago, and I suppose she thought it would be nice for me.’

‘And does she treat you well?’

‘She is a sweet lady,’ I said, feeling a rush of guilt as I spoke. ‘Indeed, I do not think I could be better treated anywhere.’

‘And her nephew? What do you think of him?’

‘Mr. Dewbrey? I think . . . ’ I paused. What did I think of him? ‘I think he is a just man,’ I said slowly. ‘I think too that he is a clever man — and he can be very agreeable company. Whatever task he had to do, I think he would do it well. He seems to manage the estate very efficiently.'

'Ah . . . yes. The estate.'

I could not understand the bitterness in his voice. Encircled by trees, we stopped and embraced. It looked as if we were going to spend the afternoon without Dryden, for once. I decided not to mention at all what he had said to Hugh. We sat down on a fallen log, and spent the next few minutes kissing. Suddenly he sat back, and looked straight into my eyes.

'I love you, Debbie.'

Like all girls I had dreamed of hearing those words — had imagined how I would reply. But I had never imagined these circumstances — meeting a young man in secret, a young man who was not received at the house where I lived.

And yet, I heard my voice answering, almost as if I had no will of my own.

'I love you, too.'

'Debbie, it was love at first sight! My darling, I know I have only spent a few hours in your company, but it would have made no difference if I had known you a lifetime!'

I was overwhelmed by his emotion, and by mine too. Love had come to me, not as I had dreamed of it, but suddenly, blindingly, it had swept into my life, and made me live a lie.

He embraced me again, very tightly.

'Debbie, you do love me, don't you? Say it again.'

'You know I do! I wish we could meet openly — I wish we could always be together.'

'We *could* always be together if we were married.'

I caught my breath in a gasp. If we were married . . . to be the wife of Hugh Stacey! He was proposing to me — me, Debbie Meredith, the companion at the Hall. There was no question of him dallying with me, he had declared his love, and followed it up by a proposal. He had behaved in a fitting manner for a gentleman. In a flash I realised that Dryden must have suspected Hugh's intentions towards me, and had warned me off for his own sake. Because certainly, if I became Hugh's wife, he would have no use for Dryden.

Hugh's wife! All the desires and ambitions which my God-fearing parents had tried to crush out of me rose to the fore.

Then I thought of the many difficulties we were faced with.

'How could we get married?' I asked helplessly. 'You do not visit the Hall, and Mrs. Dewbrey would not permit me to see you, I'm sure. And Mr. Dewbrey . . . '

Hugh's mouth twisted unpleasantly.

'Yes, there is *Mr.* Dewbrey,' he said sneeringly. 'The fine gentleman.'

I said nothing. I was too troubled by this enmity which certainly was not going to help me become Hugh's wife. When he spoke again his voice was gentle.

'For the time being we will say nothing, Debbie. I would like to take you up to Swalewell Keep, but there is no time in the afternoons.'

'Does your uncle know about me?' I asked.

'No. Uncle Roger is a recluse — he shuts himself up in his study for hours at a time. He is not unkind, just remote. Things are difficult for us, Debbie, but difficulties can always be surmounted if two people love each other. Trust me, and I will think what to do. In the meantime, we will continue to keep our meetings secret.'

'That time I first saw you,' I said. 'With whom had you been staying?'

He looked startled. 'Why do you ask? Very old friends, if you must know.'

'It's just that you lead a much quieter life than I thought you did when I first met you.'

He did not appear very pleased with this remark. He passed his hand across his head in a nervous movement.

'You have quite recovered from that chill, haven't you?' I asked, suddenly concerned. He did look paler than usual.

'Yes, I am quite well.'

He kissed me again.

'Did Dr. Denton visit you when you were ill?' I persisted.

'He did,' was the reply, after a slight pause.

'We often entertain him at the Hall.'

'Indeed? He does not enter Swalewell Keep except in a professional capacity,' said Hugh stiffly.

I realised the pride which lay behind that remark. The Staceys considered themselves infinitely superior to the Dewbreys — they were above entertaining a country doctor. And yet, Hugh wanted to marry me . . .

'That old man, Wilkins,' I said. 'The one who lives in that cottage by the river . . . '

I felt I had to ask Hugh about this.

'Yes? What about him?'

'He shouted 'Caldecott' at me — don't you remember, that morning before you were ill?'

He stood up, and drew me to my feet.

'I assure you, sweetheart, nobody takes the least notice of anything old Wilkins says and does. He's a bit odd.'

Arms entwined we began to walk back towards the Beck. I saw the familiar figure of Dryden strolling along the river bank. Vexation drove out all other thoughts.

'Can't we have one afternoon without Dryden?' I burst out.

'Well, it scarcely matters now, you're going back in any case,' Hugh pointed out. I decided to say nothing further, and to treat Dryden as though he had never warned me away. He greeted me impersonally; I wondered what he was thinking.

At tea time I was unable to eat anything, which was not surprising. Hugh Stacey had told me he loved me; he had talked of marriage, and my head was whirling with confused and wonderful ideas. It was an effort to draw my thoughts away from

Hugh, and concentrate on what my employer was saying.

'Alec mentioned having a ride over to the Campions tomorrow morning, and taking you, if I could spare you. I said I thought it could be arranged.'

'That is very kind of you.'

I hoped to meet Hugh in the afternoon, so it would be quite a strenuous day, riding and rowing. It was fortunate that I had always been an active girl.

The following morning I sat on Pansy, and patted her head gently. She pawed the cobbled yard, impatient to be off. Mr. Dewbrey mounted Sorrel, and we rode round the house and down the long drive together. I could see that he was having to hold Sorrel in; even with his master in the saddle the horse seemed skittish and unreliable.

He shook his head, his eyes rolling wildly.

I gave a little cry of fear, to Alec Dewbrey's surprise.

'What is wrong, Miss Meredith?'

'It's Sorrel — I don't like him — I don't trust him. If he ever got the bit between his teeth . . . '

Mr. Dewbrey smiled reassuringly. 'He won't — not with me on his back. He's just high spirited. It's a quality which I admire, anyway.'

'You mean in horses?'

'Not necessarily just in horses.'

How beautiful the countryside looked as we rode through it together. My companion looked splendid on horseback; I could not help thinking that Miss Campion would envy me my escort. Had they a secret understanding, or did his heart lie elsewhere? *Had* he a heart in fact, or was he indifferent to women; a born bachelor, a man's man? It did not seem impossible.

We came to some crossroads where a very old inn, 'The Gaping Goose', stood. I do not know what made me glance into the yard at the back of it, but I was astonished at what I saw. There were several men with horses, and among them Hugh Stacey and

Dryden. What would they be there for? Men only frequented such places to drink, I supposed.

'There seems to be quite a lot of activity going on at that inn — in the back, I mean,' I said cautiously.

'Possibly. It is a place with a bad reputation, Miss Meredith. It is rumoured that cock-fighting goes on there — and that's illegal, as you probably know. But it's a sport, so called, which has gone on for centuries. People turn a blind eye to many things in the country . . . there are other reasons, too, why 'The Gaping Goose' has a bad name.'

He broke off as if he had said enough. I was overcome with a feeling of repugnance at the idea that Hugh could find pleasure in such a cruel and vicious sport, if sport it could be called.

At Clovelly Manor we were shown into the drawing-room, where Mrs. Campion and her daughter greeted us kindly. We were served with biscuits and madeira wine. During the conversation which ensued, and in which I took little part, Miss Campion mentioned a Mr. Barnstaple several times. She had been introduced to this gentleman, I gathered, while staying with her aunt. I could tell she was trying to rouse some reaction from Mr. Dewbrey by mentioning this Mr. Barnstaple, but he remained politely indifferent.

'Penelope, dear,' her mother put in. 'Remember we were going to discuss the final arrangements for the garden party with Alec.'

'Yes, of course, Mama. It's a week next Saturday as you know, Alec. You will help, won't you?'

'I am only too happy to put myself at your disposal, ladies,' said Mr. Dewbrey gallantly. 'You are having a ball in the evening, I understand.'

'Yes, we have hired musicians for it. Don't forget you promised to make treacle toffee, Miss Meredith,' said Mrs. Campion.

We stayed for about an hour. I could see Penelope was loth to let Mr.

Dewbrey go, but eventually she waved us off.

My head ached that afternoon as I rowed downstream.

'Hugh,' I said, as we sat on the bank with our arms around each other, 'if it so happened that we were unable to meet for any reason, how would we keep in touch?'

'If that should happen — well, your letters are not censored, are they, my darling?'

'Oh, no, of course not! I get letters from my parents and friends every week.'

'Then if it ever did happen, I would write, and we would make arrangements to see each other, never fear.'

The day had somehow depressed me, although the warmth and tenderness of Hugh's presence was reassuring. I could not bring myself to mention it, but I could not altogether dismiss from my mind the possibility that he had seen a cock-fight that morning. Although he had asked me to consider myself engaged to him, part of his life seemed very secret. Admittedly, he had told me some things. He had told me about his parents' death during his childhood, and of his life with his hermit-like bachelor uncle. Although I still did not care for Dryden, from what Hugh had told me his life would have been bleak indeed without his companionship.

'But, Hugh, if we do get married . . . '

'We will get married,' he said confidently, kissing me.

'Well, when we do, you won't want Dryden, will you?'

There was a silence, during which he looked uncomfortable.

'But Hugh, you won't?'

'We will get married,' he said confidently, kissing me.

'Well, when we do, you won't want Dryden, will you?'

There was a silence, during which he looked uncomfortable.

'But Hugh, you won't?'

'Debbie, dearest,' he said at last, 'we can think of all these things later. You're making an issue out of a matter of small importance.'

It did not seem so to me, but I realised that it would be silly to start arguing about such things when we were only able to spend a short while in each other's company. I told Hugh that I had a headache, and felt tired. I could not have rowed upstream quickly that afternoon, so I left earlier than usual.

I had asked him if he would be at the garden party, but he merely said that he was not interested in such things. He appeared to take no part at all in village activities. If I became his wife — a thought which filled me with rapture and disbelief — would I live remote and secluded in that old Norman building which I had only seen from a distance? It seemed unreal, and yet he had told me we would be married.

As I rowed upstream I had the satisfaction of knowing that for one afternoon at least, Dryden had not appeared. Perhaps it was because I had left earlier than usual, or perhaps Hugh had told him not to come. There was no one about near the boathouse, either, but as I glanced upstream I saw Tulloch in the distance, standing outside his cottage. There was another man with him too — recognisable as being Alec Dewbrey. I had an unpleasant feeling they were both watching me. I moored the boat, and walked slowly back to the Hall. Everything was getting so complicated.

I had promised to stay with Mrs. Dewbrey a twelve-month, anyway. Not being able to meet openly would be a test for our love.

I intended to disregard all Alec Dewbrey had said about my being under his care. He could not stop me from falling in love, nor other people from loving me.

Meanwhile I would have to be very careful not to give myself away. Mrs. Dewbrey seemed very aware of my moods, and I knew that her nephew was keenly observant. I must take care not to appear too dreamy, nor abstracted, nor secretly worried. Certainly things were not going to be easy for me.

For the next few days the weather remained bright and warm, and I rowed downstream to see Hugh every afternoon.

Dryden still appeared at intervals; his manner was correctly civil towards me. One afternoon we strolled in the woods, and sat down on a fallen log.

'Debbie, I love you so much,' said Hugh.

He kissed me so hard, and held me so tightly that I felt a little twinge of fear in spite of my love for him. I knew perfectly well that it was wrong to be with a gentleman unchaperoned, and to my consternation he was beginning to behave in a rather unseemly manner. For once, perhaps, I would have been pleased to see Dryden.

'Hugh, please,' I gasped, pushing away. 'I can't go back to Ditchford Hall with my face all red.'

He laughed, and released me suddenly.

'Of course not,' he said. 'Your good friend Dewbrey might wonder where you had been.'

'Don't be like that,' I begged. 'You know I don't wish to arouse any suspicion that I row down the river to see you.'

'Of course you don't.'

As we sat there in the dappled sunlight, a brightly beautiful butterfly hovered round my foot, and fluttered up onto my shoulder, attracted probably by my yellow dress.

I gave a little cry, as with a swift movement Hugh had imprisoned it in his hand. I was speechless with horror as he produced a pin from his pocket, and impaled the creature, wings still a-flutter, on his lapel.

'Hugh!' I cried. 'Let it go — please let it go!'

'Too late,' he said calmly. 'It is dying — it will look very pretty mounted — a

Purple Emperor.'

I stood up, and made as if to go. The next moment his arms were round me again.

'Debbie, darling! I know I said I wouldn't catch any more butterflies, but I couldn't resist this one, it is so beautiful . . . '

The appeal in his voice, the charm of his long-lashed blue eyes made the incident of the butterfly seem unimportant. Arms entwined, we walked back to the river bank together. To my relief Dryden was not there.

Hugh was just helping me into the boat when we both noticed a man on horseback on the opposite side of Swalewell Beck. It was Alec Dewbrey, mounted, not on Sorrel, but on the gentle tempered Daisy.

'Hugh! I've been seen!' I gasped, feeling momentarily sick with shock and fear.

'Don't appear too disturbed; just row back as usual,' said Hugh hurriedly. 'Handle things discreetly — I will write you, never fear. He shan't come between us — remember I love you.'

He turned on his heel and made off in the direction of the Keep. Trembling, I grasped the oars and began to row back.

Mr. Dewbrey had not spoken; he had merely looked, but I had the awful feeling that he had been waiting there for me to appear.

As I rowed back he urged Daisy into a jogtrot along the path by the river. I knew beyond any doubt that he was going to meet me at the boathouse, and forbid me to row down Swalewell Beck again. By the time I brought the boat in to the landing stage, he was dismounted and waiting for me. One look at his grim, set face filled me with fresh dismay.

'I would like to have a talk with you, Miss Meredith,' he said, his voice icy.

'Would you, sir?' I asked, as coolly as I could. 'I am afraid I have little time to spare at the moment, as Mrs. Dewbrey will be expecting me to take tea with her very shortly.'

He glanced at his watch.

'What I have to say will not take long. I will walk back to the house with you.'

I patted Daisy, trying to appear unconcerned. My companion picked up the reins and led her along as we walked back through the grounds.

'I do not know how long you have been sneaking out to meet Stacey — probably almost right from first coming here. In any event, you are to discontinue meeting him immediately. I have told you I am responsible for your welfare — and it is not in your best interests to have anything to do with him. You will not take a boat out and row downstream to see him again.'

'Why not?' I asked, with as much insolence as I could muster.

'Because I say not. And I do not wish my aunt to know anything about this . . . '

'What do you mean, not in my best interests?' I asked. 'How do you know being friendly with him is not in my best interests? Because of some silly feud between two families? Because *you* don't approve of the Staceys it doesn't mean I should adopt your attitude . . . '

'What do you know about such matters? How do you know to what dangers you are exposing yourself, sneaking away like a kitchen maid to meet him? What would your parents think?'

My first fear had gone now; anger and indignation had taken its place. I forgot Hugh's talk of discretion.

'Suppose I said Mr. Stacey had asked me to marry him?' I asked recklessly. 'What would you say to that?'

Alec Dewbrey gave a disbelieving little smile.

'I should say you were extremely foolish to believe him, if he has indeed mentioned marriage.'

'I consider myself betrothed to him.'

'Do you indeed? In that case you are even more innocent and naive than I thought. I have reason to believe that Hugh Stacey will never marry — and anyway, what gain would it be to him to marry you?'

I was trembling with indignation, although he had after all only put into words the doubts which had assailed me from time to time.

'He finds me pleasing — he regards me highly,' I said, quite breathless with anger. 'It is possible for a man to love a woman without any thought of gain . . . '

'Oh I quite agree that it is possible — possible with some men, but not, I fear, with Stacey. You think he will marry you for your so-charming self alone, Miss Meredith? He will not marry at all, least of all a young woman in your position. No, I am not being insulting — you may be my aunt's companion, but that does not blind me to the fact that you can hold your own with any of the fashionable beauties the Riding has to offer. But concerning Stacey — he has no good intentions towards you, only bad ones. He will not harm you while I am here to prevent it though.'

I suddenly felt quite weak and breathless. I stopped walking and leaned against a tree. Arguing was not the way to deal with Mr. Dewbrey — far better to let him think that I would defer to his authority.

'Are you all right, Miss Meredith?' he asked, and there was concern in his voice.

'Yes,' I said distantly. 'Please don't upbraid me any further concerning my behaviour, although I'm sure your motives are of the best. I can see that I am not free to do as I wish during the time I remain here as Mrs. Dewbrey's companion. You will have no further cause for complaint.'

'Then let us forget the matter,' he said, sounding relieved. 'I realise that you are young and trusting, and away from your parents' guidance for the first time. There is much to occupy you here — you will be wise to put all thoughts of Stacey out of your mind.'

'Please excuse me now, sir,' I said, in

a suitably meek voice. 'Mrs. Dewbrey does not like me to be late for tea.'

He stood to one side and let me make my way to the house without saying anything further. Outwardly at least I had deferred to him. Back in my room I pondered over the things he had said concerning Hugh; that he would never marry, and least of all to a young woman in my position.

How dare Alec Dewbrey be so presumptuous! And yet in the next breath he had said that I could hold my own with any of the fashionable beauties the Riding had to offer. I looked at myself in the mirror; at my blue-green eyes, rounded cheeks and pointed chin. I knew that Hugh would get in touch with me, and that somehow we would see each other again. I rang for hot water, and as I made my toilet I continued thinking over the events of the afternoon. Other men seemed inclined to interfere between myself and Hugh. I thought of Dryden and his warning; he was thinking of his own very pleasant position at Swalewell Keep. In Alec Dewbrey's case (apart from the fact that he was ill-disposed towards Hugh), being somewhat indifferent to the opposite sex himself, it probably irked him that other men were not.

How childish, I thought, as I dabbed cologne on my wrists. However, my mind was abruptly taken off my own affairs, as I found Mrs. Dewbrey far from well at tea time. She complained of a pain in her chest, but said she did not need the doctor, only a good rest. Alice helped her to bed, and I told her I would sit with her, and have dinner sent up for us both.

She looked pleased.

'That is a good idea, Debbie; it means Alec will dine alone, though.'

'I am sure he will not mind in the circumstances,' I said smoothly. I was genuinely sorry that his aunt was not well, but I was pleased that I would not see him for the rest of the day.

In this I was mistaken, as he came to

see her, concern very plain on his face. He suggested getting the doctor.

'I've no pain, now, Alec, I just feel tired.'

In spite of being so taken up with myself and Hugh, I felt a little pang of remorse, sitting in that luxurious room. Mrs. Dewbrey was so kind to me — she would be very upset if she knew about my secret meetings with a member of a family she was not friendly with. I still intended to defy Alec Dewbrey, though; I did not see why his prejudices should be allowed to affect my life. I had a right to love and be loved — had not Hugh Stacey told me so?

Mr. Dewbrey was standing looking through the window, frowning. Horatio put his head on the bed, and gazed sadly at Mrs. Dewbrey. I sat embroidering a cushion cover.

Abruptly, Alec Dewbrey turned round.

'Have you seen Mrs. Tukes about the treacle toffee, Miss Meredith? The garden party is drawing near.'

'I will do what is necessary, sir,' I

said, in what I hoped was a cool and dignified manner. 'But I may not be there to sell it — I shall not leave Mrs. Dewbrey unless she improves.'

'But of course I shall be well, my dear,' came her voice from the bed. 'Really, I'm getting too much fuss made of me altogether. Probably I am not really over that chill yet.'

After about a quarter of an hour, Mr. Dewbrey left us, and I sat embroidering in silence.

After some time, to my surprise I noticed that his aunt had fallen asleep. I walked over to the window, and looked out on the loveliness of a summer evening. Restlessness welled up in me. I felt the love between Hugh and myself was strong enough to survive setbacks and separation, but even so, I would have been pleased if things could have been different.

I decided there was no need for me to stay in the bedroom all evening. Instead, I would visit the Servants' Hall, and mention the treacle toffee to

Mrs. Tukes. I would tell Alice her mistress was asleep.

The library door was closed when I walked past it, but I heard the sound of men's voices coming from within. Evidently Mr. Dewbrey had company for the evening.

In the Servants' Hall I explained to Mrs. Tukes about the treacle toffee.

'Why, of course, if you want to make it yourself, miss, I'll see everything's ready when you need it,' she said smiling.

I withdrew, and went to my room with the intention of writing some letters. It was quite by accident that, some time later, I looked through the window and saw a man leaving the house on horseback. His mount was a Cleveland Bay, and I could not fail to recognise the thickset figure of the rider.

It was Dryden.

13

I felt almost faint as I picked up my letters from the oak table in the entrance hall. I recognised my mother's writing — and Georgina's writing — but there was a third envelope addressed to me in another hand.

With my heart beating wildly, I took it to my room.

'My darling Debbie,' it ran — 'I hope with all my heart that things did not go too badly with you, after you had been seen by Dewbrey. No doubt you got a stern warning not to row down the river, or see me again. I have a plan, though. Have you the courage to slip out next Tuesday and meet me at night? I know it will mean you rowing across the river in the dark, but I can think of no other way. You would not have to row downstream, as I will wait for you opposite the boathouse at midnight. If you have the courage to do this, please wear pink to church on Sunday. If it rains heavily I will not expect you . . .'

There was more, assuring me of his devotion, but asking me not to answer his letter. For a moment I felt as though things were getting too much for me. I had wondered repeatedly what Dryden's business had been at Ditchford Hall, and I was determined to mention it to Hugh when I did see him. But to sneak out at night in the summer darkness and row across the river . . . it would take some courage as well as some organising.

By an odd chance, I would be in the kitchen tomorrow making treacle toffee. It meant I would be able to have a good look round, and see if getting out at night was a feasible proposition. Naturally, I longed to write to Hugh, but I had to be content in the thought that I would see him in church.

Mrs. Dewbrey seemed quite recovered, and the following afternoon I presented myself in Mrs. Tukes' kitchen, to make the toffee.

The kitchen was dominated by a huge range, fitted with ovens and boilers, at each side of which was a comfortable Windsor armchair. There were deal tables, a dresser, kitchen chairs, and batteries of iron and copper saucepans, frying pans, skillets and sieves hanging up.

Mrs. Tukes handed me a white apron, and a new maid, Janet, was told to help me. Horatio lay under a table, his head between his paws. I knew from a remark that Mrs. Dewbrey had once made that the dog slept in the kitchen.

The idea of creeping out of the house late at night sent icy shivers down my spine. If Horatio was in the kitchen he would probably let me go quietly enough, but I would have to get back without having him bark. I could get him to come out with me, of course, he never turned down the chance of a walk.

It seemed to me the best plan. If I took the dog with me I would have no fear of going out at midnight; moreover, there would be no danger of him barking on my return.

I greased a large, shallow tin, to pour the first batch of toffee into it. I looked at the many keys hanging in the kitchen, and at the row of bells. There was a key in the stout oak door, and beyond was the scullery where the maids cleaned the pans. There, too, was the wash-house with its coppers and tubs.

Leaving Janet busy with the toffee, I walked into the back, and looked at the outer door. To my relief, the key was in place. That would save me having to find out which key belonged to it. There was a bolt at the bottom of the door.

I hoped with all my heart that it was not stiff, but I had an idea it wouldn't be. I had a feeling that as an old and trusted servant Mrs. Tukes probably had the responsibility of locking up these premises, even though the butler locked up elsewhere.

The Saturday of the garden party

dawned, fair and sunny. In spite of thinking constantly about Hugh, and the many problems connected with him, I could not help feeling a certain pleasure in the day that lay ahead. I selected a pretty muslin dress, and a floppy sunbonnet to protect my complexion.

Janet and I had weighed out the toffee, and put it into pokes of white paper. Our ball gowns were in Alice's care, she travelled with us to Clovelly Manor, as we would need her services before the gaiety of the evening began.

A marquee for refreshments had been erected; there was a coconut shy, stalls for the sale of various goods, and a variety of things to amuse the children.

Mrs. Campion and her daughter greeted us graciously, and we were introduced to a number of people who were there as house guests. My toffee was received enthusiastically by Mrs. Campion — she tasted a piece and declared it delicious.

'This is your stall, Miss Meredith,' she said, leading me towards one. It was so warm that Alec Dewbrey had discarded his jacket as he supervised the setting up of various stalls.

'I hope you are not too exposed to the sun,' he said.

'Not at all. I'm wearing a sunbonnet,' I replied, setting out the pokes of toffee.

'They look very professional,' he remarked.

'Alec has worked so hard,' said Mrs. Campion, as he moved away. 'He enjoys anything like this — no wonder he is popular in the village. My kitchen staff are busy, as you can imagine, what with the garden party and the house-guests, and of course, the ball tonight. Ram Singh has his hands full — and then Penelope teased the poor man by telling him that we were going to have him in a tent telling fortunes. She is mischievous at times.'

I smiled, but an unpleasant memory stirred in me. Ram Singh's soft, slurred voice murmuring a warning about my future. People who would work evil . . . in spite of the warmth of the day, I shivered. Then I dismissed it as nonsense. Ram Singh had probably enjoyed the idea of frightening an English miss.

The garden party was an unqualified success. I stood selling toffee to round-eyed village children, and put the farthings in a glass jar.

'You run your stall very efficiently, Miss Meredith,' remarked Mr. Dewbrey, sampling a poke of toffee during the afternoon.

'I'm used to this sort of thing,' I explained, counting my takings.

'And you like it?' For a moment I was startled; the question was so unexpected.

'Like it? Why, I don't know, sir,' I said slowly. 'I suppose I was brought up to do this sort of thing, so I just do it.'

'I see. What is a novelty to some people is but a run of the mill duty to you.'

Had there been sarcasm in his voice,

I would have resented that remark, but he spoke gently, and as though he understood what I meant. I caught sight of Miss Campion flitting around, looking delightful, and being absolutely charming. She was taking care not to do any work, though. Alec Dewbrey's glance followed mine, and I saw a faintly amused expression in his eye. I had a feeling that he had noticed the same thing.

In spite of my recent brush with him, I felt a reluctant respect. She caught his eyes and smiled enchantingly at him, showing her feelings all too plainly.

After a while I sat down on the stool he had given me earlier in the afternoon. I had sold out of toffee, and the shadows were lengthening on the grass. Mrs. Dewbrey was sitting on a cane chair in the shade, talking to the vicar's wife. Tea and lemonade were being served; by general consent everyone was having a rest.

When evening came, and Alice was helping me dress for the ball, I found myself looking forward to it. There was much chatter in the bedrooms, which were full of ladies and their maids scurrying about with smelling salts and curling tongs. Mrs. Dewbrey had insisted that I should have a ball gown made, and that as it was my first one, it should be white.

It was of figured silk, very stylishly cut, with the lowest neckline I had ever worn. It moulded my figure like a second skin; I was rather glad Mama couldn't see me in it. I had heard her deplore the passing of the crinoline, and I understood why as I looked at the outlines of my body in the mirror.

Although plain at the front, the dress fell in elaborate tiers behind, frilled, and trimmed with red roses.

Mrs. Dewbrey had lent me a single string of pearls, saying that was all I needed. She had also made me the gift of a very lovely Japanese fan; I was touched by her overwhelming generosity.

Miss Campion was radiant in a ball

gown of sapphire blue. It was hard for me to define her attitude towards me. I knew that she was jealous because I lived under the same roof as Mr. Dewbrey, but the fact that I was a mere companion saved me from any real demonstration of her feelings. I was not in a position to be treated as a serious rival, rather, her sweet but slightly patronising manner was designed to let me know my 'place', even though the eccentric Mrs. Dewbrey appeared to treat me like a daughter. A number of people were foregathered in the drawing-room, including a Mr. Roger Barnstaple, the gentleman whom Miss Campion had talked about when I had visited Clovelly Manor with Mr. Dewbrey. He was about thirty-five, and quite distinguished looking, if rather nervous in his manner.

He could scarcely take his eyes off her, but I knew she cared nothing for him. His presence there was a move on her part to let Mr. Dewbrey see that other men found her attractive. Later in the evening we withdrew to the gallery for dancing. I sat beside Mrs. Dewbrey in my low-cut gown, my long kid ball gloves, and my borrowed pearls. I did not sit for long, though. I was slightly surprised — and pleased — to find there was quite a rush from gentlemen who were eager to book dances.

In spite of my love for Hugh, I found myself enjoying the ball immensely. Mrs. Dewbrey appeared pleased at my popularity; almost I forgot that I was a paid companion.

Alec Dewbrey booked a dance, to my embarrassment. I knew that Miss Campion was watching as we took the floor together. It was a waltz, and he danced beautifully, which I thought rather strange for a man who seemed indifferent to such pastimes.

No, that was untrue. He was not indifferent to them, he was . . . he was . . .

'You dance well, Miss Meredith,' he said.

I was thankful for the hours I had spent practising with Georgina.

'So do you, sir.' He smiled without speaking.

'Miss Campion dances very well, too,' I observed, somewhat slyly.

'She has all the accomplishments considered desirable in a gentlewoman,' was the rather puzzling reply.

'And her gown is beautiful,' I went on.

'Indeed?'

Something in his voice stopped me from commenting any further about Miss Campion.

'You are not short of partners for the evening,' he said.

No, I was not short of partners, and his remark about my being able to hold my own with any of the beauties of the Riding came back to me. The waltz ended, and his eyes swept over me with a curiously personal gaze.

'Your ball gown is too low,' he said abruptly, and escorted me back to my seat beside his aunt. He bowed very formally, and left me fanning myself, angrily indignant. He had put into words what I had secretly known myself. The man was impertinent — no — insolent, I told myself. He thought he had the right to interfere with my life, dictate to me about my friendships, and even to comment on my clothes.

14

My face looked demurely back at me in the mirror, as I adjusted my pink bonnet, ready for going to church. My heart was fluttering at the thought of seeing Hugh again.

I caught sight of him with Dryden and his uncle entering the church just as we reached the gates.

The emotions that filled me were almost unbearable, but I had learnt to keep my face impassive when I was with Mr. Dewbrey. He was all too observant, and I wanted to play my part successfully.

I felt rather than saw Hugh's presence in that church. We exchanged one swift, passionate glance, which told both of us all we needed to know.

The next two days were hot and sunny, and on Tuesday night I sat up late writing letters in my bedroom. I was trying to keep calm, but I was both frightened and excited. I had my hooded cloak ready on the bed, and at a quarter to twelve I put it on, and picked up the candle.

I no longer troubled to lock my bedroom door — the memory of that ghostly kiss having faded somewhat — and as I opened it my shadow loomed up, large and mysterious against the wall. The house was silent. I walked along the corridors and descended the staircase, pausing to listen occasionally. I had no idea at what hour Mr. Dewbrey retired; it probably varied.

At last I stood outside the kitchen door. With a quick movement I opened it, hissing 'Shush!' at Horatio. He stood up, making tiny growling noises, and wagging his tail uneasily. He was fond of sweetmeats, although his master disliked him having many, but I had a few biscuits with me, and fed him them immediately.

Then I set the candle down on the

dresser, and patted his head reassuringly. The familiar objects in the room became identifiable.

To my relief Horatio did not bark; he was puzzled by my appearance in the night, and he seemed to be waiting for my next move.

'Come on, Horatio,' I murmured. 'Good dog.'

With him close beside me I unlocked the kitchen door, and went through the scullery and the rooms and passages beyond. I set down the candlestick in front of the outer door, drew the heavy bolt, and unlocked it. Now that I had gone so far with my plan, and had Horatio under control, I was filled with a kind of cool daring. I drew the dog outside with me, closed the door silently, and locked it, putting the key in the pocket of my cloak.

To my relief Horatio walked quietly along beside me; the hours I had spent making friends with him were certainly being rewarded. Without him I would have been fearful indeed. The outbuildings loomed up eerily in the moonlight, and behind them the orchard. I found the footpath and walked along with Horatio at my heels. At last, through the trees I saw the gleam of the river ahead; I quickened my pace, and moments later I was at the boathouse. As I unmoored the boat I could hear a nightingale singing, filling the moonlit silence with its sweet, plaintive song.

'Come on, Horatio,' I said, and his big body thudded into the boat. 'Lie down.'

I began to row across the expanse of water. There was a whistle from the bank opposite, and I drew a gasping sigh of relief. He was there!

A few moments later the bank rose in front of me, and with it the figure of Hugh in the moonlight. He helped me out of the boat, mooring it on a tree which was growing half in the water.

Horatio jumped out after me, and stood snarling uncompromisingly at Hugh.

'Shush!' I hissed crossly.

'You've brought a dog — it's Dewbrey's hound,' he said, sounding none too pleased himself. 'Why have you, Debbie?'

'I had to! He sleeps in the kitchen — if he wasn't with me he would bark and rouse the whole household,' I explained.

'I daren't touch you! He'll put his teeth into me if I do.' Hugh's voice was morose. I felt like crying — I had planned and schemed to get out and meet him, and nothing was going right.

'Sit down — down!' I whispered fiercely, patting Horatio's head. I managed to coax him into a sitting position, but he continued to growl softly. However, I was able to slip my hand in Hugh's, and feel the answering pressure from his.

'He'll be all right in a few minutes, Hugh — give him time to get used to you,' I said. 'It's been lonely and terrible without you.'

'My darling! I've been living for this

moment. I knew you would not fail me.'

Cautiously, with Horatio watching warily, he drew me into his arms.

'What did Dewbrey say when he saw you with me on the bank?' he asked eagerly.

'He forbade me to see you — to row down the river, or meet you under any circumstances.'

'I expected that. What else did he say?'

'He said that you had no good intentions towards me! And then — I know we were supposed to be keeping it a secret — don't be angry with me, Hugh — I told him we considered ourselves engaged, and he laughed! He said that if I believed that, then I was even more innocent than he had thought. He said that you would not marry anyone, least of all a girl in my position . . . '

For a moment I was unable to go on. Hugh's grip on me tightened.

'Go on Debbie.'

'It's not true, is it? You did mean

what you said about us getting married?'

'I meant it all right.'

I clung to him, relief and happiness welling up in me.

'There's another thing, Hugh. That same evening I saw a man ride away from the house, and I'm positive it was Dryden.'

'It may well have been.'

'But what was he doing there? Would he be talking to Mr. Dewbrey about us?'

'Most unlikely. Apart from giving me companionship, Dryden looks after a number of things at Swalewell Keep. He would be seeing Dewbrey about something concerning the estate, I have no doubt.'

'But I don't understand what concern your land would be to him . . . '

'Debbie, you don't understand a lot of things,' said Hugh, and there was an edge of impatience in his voice. 'Our land is divided by Swalewell Beck, but there are all sorts of things which crop up from time to time. He would be there on business — dismiss the matter from your mind.'

I was only too eager to do this. Hugh slipped his hand under my cloak; I felt his touch like fire on my bare neck. I gave a little gasp, and Horatio stood up, growling.

'That damn dog,' whispered Hugh.

I was glad I had him with me, though. Hugh's caresses had rendered me almost faint; fear of being swept off my feet rose within me.

'I dare not stay long,' I whispered.

'Debbie, you'll come tomorrow?'

'Yes . . . but we can't go on like this. I can't keep on meeting you secretly — creeping out of the house . . . '

'I've thought of that. My darling, have you the courage to meet me and run away with me to get married?'

'Run away!'

The enormity of the suggestion nearly bowled me over. To sneak out and leave behind my responsibilities; my duty to Mrs. Dewbrey and to my parents? To flaunt my defiance in Alec Dewbrey's face, and prove him wrong about Hugh's intentions?

A thrill of fear ran right through me, but the wonderful, tantalising prospect of being Hugh's wife was stronger than fear; stronger than the sense of duty which had been instilled in me from childhood.

'Say yes, Debbie! I will arrange everything.'

'Yes,' I heard myself saying, from a long way off. 'Yes, I will, Hugh. I love you — arrange what you please. You know I trust you . . . '

We discussed things for a few more minutes, and then I rowed back across the Beck. As I moored the boat at the landing stage there was a faint, farewell whistle from the bank opposite, and then silence. Hugh was on his way back to Swalewell Keep.

I could tell Horatio was eager to be home. And in spite of my joy at being in Hugh's arms again, I too felt relief that we were on our way back. Ditchford

Hall was a welcome sight.

Silently I opened the great oaken door; it swung back on its hinges, and revealed the candle where I had left it. I turned and locked the door behind me, bolting it carefully. After the chill freshness of the night air, the damp, soapy smell of the wash-house was very noticeable. In the kitchen, I patted Horatio's head coaxingly, to make him lie on the mat.

At last, safe in my bedroom, I yawned with weariness as I closed the door and set down the candle. I undressed and tumbled into bed, and yet, tired though I was, sleep would not come. I relived the time I had spent in Hugh Stacey's arms. To take this tremendous step; to defy everyone and marry Hugh without consulting anyone . . . no, I would never dare.

And yet, Hugh's pleading voice, the love he felt for me, and I for him . . .

The next thing I knew, Alice was knocking at the door.

'I don't want ringlets today, Alice,' I

said, as she helped me with my toilet. 'I want a plain style for a change.'

'Very well, miss.'

Her deft hands were busy; before long my hair was pinned up in neat coils. Somehow I felt that Mr. Dewbrey would not suspect a girl with a severe hair style and cotton gown of doing anything as daring as sneaking out at night to meet a man.

He was at the breakfast table, and greeted me pleasantly, as usual.

'You look different this morning, Miss Meredith,' he said.

I was on my guard immediately at his remark. Horatio had greeted me with a short bark, and now lay contentedly under the table.

'I assure you, sir, I have not changed,' I said, helping myself to a dish of devilled kidneys.

'It's your hair,' he went on, his dark eyes twinkling in an oddly disconcerting way. 'One gets used to a certain style, and then, hey presto! the lady changes it.'

'And you approve, sir?' I asked, somewhat pertly.

'Do you care about my approval?' His voice was serious now.

Somehow I could not answer him, I merely smiled, and ate my breakfast. He would certainly not approve of my behaviour. Although I was contemplating eloping with Hugh, in my heart I did not wish to upset the Dewbreys. This dark, enigmatic man could be so charming, but he had laid his commands on me, and expected to be obeyed. I resented that, and yet, I felt that I wanted, if not his approval, his understanding.

'You are thoughtful, Miss Meredith.'

'And you are observant, sir.'

He smiled. 'These mumbled eggs are excellent.'

'So are the kidneys.'

'Do you intend to ride this morning, Miss Meredith?'

'I do not know what plans Mrs. Dewbrey may have.'

'If she has no particular plans,

perhaps you would like to ride into the village with me.'

'Thank you, sir. I will let you know.'

I rode into the village with him, but after luncheon I was overcome with weariness.

Mrs. Dewbrey asked if the ride had tired me.

'I trust not,' said her nephew, setting down his cup of coffee. 'Otherwise, when the hunting season begins, Miss Meredith will find it very fatiguing.'

I had not known that I would be expected to follow the hounds, but Mrs. Dewbrey did not appear surprised at that remark.

I reflected that before the hunting season began, I might be Hugh Stacey's bride.

That night I crept out to meet him again, although I knew that I would certainly not be able to do it every night.

Horatio accompanied me again, although he was still suspicious of Hugh. Before I left him, my love took a small package out of his pocket.

'A betrothal gift for you, Debbie — take great care of it — it has been in the Stacey family for years.'

'What is it?' I whispered excitedly.

'Wait and see,' he said tenderly. Beneath my cloak his caressing hands slipped it down the front of my dress for safety.

'You will soon be my bride,' he murmured. 'If we can continue seeing each other through the summer, we can run away together in August. I shall be twenty-one then, and I will come into my inheritance.'

After a tender farewell, I again crept back into the house with Horatio. As soon as I was safely in my room, I pulled out the package from my bosom, and opened it. It was the most exquisite necklace; in the lamplight I saw the glow of red stones. Were they garnets, or rubies? A sigh broke from me. I was so divinely happy — and so very unhappy, at the same time.

15

In the morning I examined Hugh's gift carefully. It was of gold filigree set with both rubies and garnets. I had never possessed anything as lovely in my life; I would never be able to wear it at Ditchford Hall, though. I imagined Alec Dewbrey's keen eyes scrutinising it. He would know it was no cheap imitation.

And yet, it was mine if I chose to wear it . . .

I twisted and turned in front of the mirror, watching the precious stones catch the light. It would be foolish to pretend that the idea of eloping did not frighten me terribly. But if I didn't run away with Hugh, where would it end? I stared through my bedroom window at the flower beds below. Once the summer had gone, I would not be able to see him, except in church.

And then — what would come then?

Dryden would have Hugh all to himself. What pressures, what influences would he bring to bear? He did not wish our friendship to continue; could our love survive under such conditions? And if it did, what would be the final outcome?

'I ask you, Debbie, to give it a twelvemonth . . . '

I turned from the window, and slowly unfastened the necklace. Dear Papa . . . I was sorry, but I was not going to give it a twelvemonth. Perhaps some day people might understand, and forgive, but I wanted to be Hugh Stacey's wife, and as soon as possible.

The days slipped by, while I led my double life. By day I was the perfect companion for Mrs. Dewbrey, painting with her, reading to her, playing the piano, or playing cribbage.

I wrote dutiful letters home, and somewhat stilted ones to Georgina, as perforce I was concealing so much which would have been of interest to her.

My social position was not clearly defined at Ditchford Hall, but certainly I was not treated like a paid companion.

There were times when Mr. Dewbrey talked freely to me about the running of the estate; occasionally too, he would discuss his aunt's health, taking it for granted that I was old enough and sensible enough to understand, and to watch her for signs of overstrain.

In my plain morning dresses, with my neatly coiled hair, I probably invited the odd confidence of this nature. After nightfall, things were different. Sometimes I would be tensed up the entire evening, waiting for midnight. I met Hugh three or four times a week, and each time, although the joy of being held in his arms made it worth while, it was no less of an ordeal.

But all things take on a routine after a while, and my clandestine meetings became part of my life. Horatio, too, knew what to expect when I appeared in the kitchen with the lighted candle.

We were having a prolonged dry spell; the weather was ideal for moonlit meetings. And each day, each week, brought my wedding nearer. Horatio would sit watchfully while Hugh clasped me in his arms and told me of the plans he had made.

It was all so simple, really. He had decided on the date of our elopement, the fifteenth of August.

I was to go as usual to meet him, only without Horatio. With my essential clothes in a valise, I would row across Swalewell Beck as usual. Hugh would join me, and we would row downstream below where the river curved.

Then we would walk across the Stacey land to Halifield, and catch the first train to Leeds, and from thence to Scotland, where, Hugh said, it would be an easy matter to get married. He did not mention Dryden, and neither did I. Evidently he accepted the idea that I would not welcome him as a third party after we were married.

'I shall, of course, write home and tell my parents not to worry,' I said, not feeling too happy about it.

'Of course, my darling. And I shall leave a note for my uncle. Once he gets used to the idea he will accept it without fuss — he's like that. But so remote, if you understand.'

'Yes . . . ' I said. I didn't really understand, but nothing seemed to matter except marrying Hugh.

'After we are married, we will go abroad for the winter, and when we return, you will be Mistress of Swalewell Keep, Debbie.'

I felt quite awed. I tried to imagine living there, on the other side of the river. How strange it would be to see Alec Dewbrey strolling with Tulloch on the land opposite. I pictured myself going to church, sitting in a different pew, and seeing the frail figure of Mrs. Dewbrey, and the stalwart one of her nephew, angry and unforgiving at her side . . . And of course — my parents. What of my parents? These were the tormenting thoughts which went through my mind, but I still went forward with my plans to elope. June and July slipped by, with long, warm days, and exciting nights. Soon it was August, and already stray leaves were breaking away and falling as the moorland breezes blew.

My love came of age, and I bought him a dressing set; brushes and shoe horn of silver. The night of the elopement came swiftly after Hugh's birthday; in no time it was upon us, and I proceeded with my part of our carefully laid plans.

* * *

I packed as much as I could carry in my smaller valise.

They were all clothes which I had brought with me to Ditchford Hall; the pretty gowns which Mrs. Dewbrey had insisted on buying for me were left in the wardrobe. I had eaten hardly anything all day. At breakfast that morning I had scarcely been able to meet Alec Dewbrey's eye, so guilty did I feel.

I had spent the afternoon in my room, packing. I had written a note to Mrs. Dewbrey, thanking her for having me at Ditchford Hall, and for being so kind. I told her that I was leaving, but that I would get in touch with my parents, and that it was not her responsibility. I added that circumstances had arisen in my life which had caused me to make big changes in my plans.

I put the note in an envelope, and placed it on the dressing table, for Alice to find in the morning, along with another envelope for her, containing a sovereign.

Rather unnecessarily Hugh had reminded me to bring the necklace; I packed it with my other valuables. The moon was full that night; we would need no lamps or lanterns, Hugh had said. When the time came, I put on my hooded cloak, picked up my valise, and crept out of my room and down the stairs as I had been doing for several weeks now. For the last time, I opened the kitchen door, and Horatio came forward, wagging his tail.

'Be quiet, good dog,' I murmured, patting his head. He followed me expectantly to the outer door. I unlocked it and drew the bolt as usual. Horatio pushed forward, but I coaxed him back by throwing a handful of biscuits into the passage. Quickly I slipped out, and closed the door behind me.

I would have to leave it unlocked, but with a watchdog like Horatio, that would not matter for one night. My heart was pounding. To be out alone at that hour was by no means a pleasant experience, apart from all the other circumstances.

Once in Hugh's arms I knew my fears would fade swiftly; I was more than glad when I reached the landing stage safely, and saw him waiting for me on the other side. I had lost a glove in my haste, missing it almost as soon as I had left the house.

For the last time I unmoored the boat. I put my valise in, and rowed across to where Hugh was waiting. Then, in the distance, I heard the sound of a dog barking. Would it be Tulloch's dog, or Horatio? By the time I had reached the opposite bank my hands were trembling so violently I could hardly row.

'Debbie! Debbie! My darling!'

I was near to weeping as Hugh steadied the boat alongside the bank, and prepared to get in.

'Come on, change over seats. I'll take the oars.'

He had a valise with him which he put in the boat, and after a few moments we were settled, with him as oarsman.

He began to row downstream with rapid strokes. The bright moonlight outlined the banks of the river, and shone on the figure of my future husband as we started out on the great adventure we had planned. A dog barked again, and I recognised the bark.

'It's Horatio!' I cried despairingly. 'Oh, Hugh, something has gone wrong! We're being followed!'

'Blast that hound!' he muttered angrily, pulling at the oars. There was more barking, much nearer this time.

'Yes, we're being followed,' he said tensely. 'I can see a rowing boat moving out onto the Beck. I'll have to row like fury a bit further down, and then abandon the boat and make for the woods.'

I could hear the frenzied anxiety in his voice, and I felt physically sick. Hugh rowed as if his life depended on it, then, as the river began to curve round, he drew into the bank. He stood up; the boat rocked alarmingly, and I gave a cry of fear.

He threw both our valises onto the bank, and stepped after them.

'Come on, Debbie.'

'What about the boat?' I asked.

'It will just have to drift downstream — I can't moor it, can I? Use your common sense.'

He seized my arm and pulled me clear of the boat, agitation making him almost rough. Of course he couldn't moor the boat — that would give away our landing place immediately.

He picked up the valises and began to hurry along, with me stumbling after him.

I was panting with fear and exertion, but we had not gone far before Hugh gave a cry of what sounded like utter despair. He dropped the valises, and I caught his hand, terror turning me cold.

A figure stood four-square in front of us, broad, menacing, complete with blackthorn walking stick. It was Dryden.

'Where are you going, Mr. Hugh?' he asked, his voice curiously authoritative. 'Shouldn't you be in your bed? And you, Miss Meredith?'

All the dislike which I felt for the man boiled over.

'Shouldn't you sir?' I asked angrily, before Hugh could speak at all.

'Come on, Mr. Hugh,' went on Dryden, a coaxing note in his voice now. 'Come on, we'll go back to the house. I'll look after Miss Meredith . . . '

'Stand aside, Dryden,' said Hugh. 'I'm twenty-one now, and I'm going to lead my own life.'

'Don't make things difficult, Mr. Hugh. Do as I say . . . '

Suddenly Hugh uttered a cry which seemed scarcely human. To my amazement and horror he sprang at Dryden, and the two men closed. It was unbelievable; nightmarish. I screamed and screamed again; in the moonlight I could see them rolling about on the ground.

'Hugh! Hugh!' I could hear my voice like a high-pitched whine, as though it didn't belong to me. They were grappling about in the clearing; Dryden was much more heavily built than

Hugh, and yet Hugh seemed to be holding his own. In the distance, through the sound of my own cries, and the noise the men were making, I could hear a dog's bark getting nearer.

Then Horatio, wet and slobbering, jumped up at me, with Alec Dewbrey close behind.

'Sit, Horatio,' he commanded brusquely. 'Sit!'

He turned to me. 'Stay here,' he said, in much the same tone. Then he hurried forward to the two men struggling on the ground. Presently I heard the most awful cries coming from Hugh — I guessed that he had recognised Alec Dewbrey.

I stood weeping, with Horatio barking beside me; had he been less well trained he would have rushed forward to defend his master, but he had been told to sit.

Then in the moonlight I could see them bending over Hugh: they were talking to each other — they were actually tying him up! I hurried forward, sobbing, my legs suddenly terribly weak. Horatio bounded forward with me, not sure what to do.

Alec Dewbrey straightened up, and called his dog to his side. Hugh lay motionless on the grass. I knelt down beside him, and looked with terror at the thin trickle of blood running from his mouth.

'Hugh! Hugh! Oh, my darling! My darling!'

I cradled his head in my arms, and covered his forehead with anguished kisses.

'He's dying!' I sobbed. 'You've killed him!'

'He'll not die, Miss Meredith,' said Dryden quietly. 'He's just knocked out. He'll be round soon . . . please go now.'

Alec Dewbrey bent down and touched my arm.

'Come on, Miss Meredith,' he said. 'The sooner we get back the better.'

'I'm not coming!' I cried. I was filled with outrage at what these two men had done.

Dryden stooped and wiped the blood away from Hugh's mouth.

'Come on, miss,' he said persuasively. 'Leave Mr. Hugh to me. I know how to handle him . . . '

'*You* know!' I cried, the strain of the night exploding in hatred of him. 'You have no right to interfere — you have no right to prevent him from going away with me! We're going to get married, do you hear? We're going to get married!'

'We're going back to Ditchford Hall,' said Alec Dewbrey, and his voice was as hard as his grip as he pulled me away.

'I've got his valise,' I heard Dryden saying. 'Yes, that's hers — it's all right, I can manage him perfectly well — yes, get her out of the way.'

Somehow my hands were prised away from Hugh's body, and I was standing on my shaky legs again.

'I told you to keep away from him, miss,' said Dryden. 'Now you go back with Mr. Dewbrey and forget all about it.'

I knew then that I was beaten. Alec Dewbrey's arm was thrust firmly through mine; in the other hand he held my valise. I tried to summon up a vestige of dignity, but the tears were rolling down my cheeks unheeded.

I turned round to give a last, agonised look at Hugh, and I saw Dryden's face in the moonlight, weary, unsmiling, and riven with pity.

Then, in a daze, I was stumbling along on the dew-wet grass, with Alec Dewbrey holding me, and Horatio at the other side. Numb with shock and despair I was led back to the river bank, where the other boat was moored. He must have heard me scream, and pulled into the side, I thought dully. The other boat would be drifting downstream . . .

I was being rowed back up Swalewell Beck now. I sat, a huddled heap in the boat, with Horatio's great warm body pressing against me. With rapid strokes Mr. Dewbrey rowed back to the boathouse. I couldn't control my frantic, hopeless sobbing. It distressed

Horatio, and he began to whine miserably.

I imagined Dryden taking Hugh back to Swalewell Keep, dazed and bleeding, with his arms and hands tied with twine. But what right had he to treat Hugh like that? Surely he would be dismissed from his post after this . . . if it hadn't been for him we would probably have given Alec Dewbrey the slip.

Silently he helped me out of the boat at the landing stage.

The three of us walked back to the house, Alec Dewbrey's arm firmly linked in mine. Despite my resentment against him I was glad of it, because my legs were weak with shock.

Back in the kitchen, I sank down into one of the Windsor armchairs. Nausea and faintness began to close in on me; everything went dark, and I seemed to be falling into bottomless blackness.

When I regained consciousness I was lying on my bed, cold perspiration running off my forehead. In the soft glow of the lamp I recognised Alec Dewbrey's face bending over me.

He was rubbing my hands, which were icy. I was shivering uncontrollably.

'Here, drink this,' he said, and his voice was surprisingly gentle. I sipped from the glass he held. It was brandy, and the burning liquid seemed to penetrate to my very nerve endings.

'You've had a bad faint, Miss Meredith. I've put your valise under the bed . . . now I'll wish you goodnight. You had better plead a headache in the morning, and stay in bed.'

He left the room, closing the door silently.

* * *

I rose for luncheon, and looked at my pale, heavy-eyed face in the mirror. Shock and fear had left their mark, but what of the future? I thought of Alec Dewbrey, and how he had witnessed everything, my hopeless love for Hugh, and my humiliation. Not only that, but he must have carried me upstairs to my room when I fainted. Then he must have brought up my valise, and the brandy.

But Hugh — my darling Hugh!

I tried to choke back a sob. The tears kept welling up in my eyes as though I had no control over them at all. Then, in the midst of my distress I remembered Mama's injunctions to be calm and dignified in the face of misfortune. I drew myself erect, and went down to the dining-room. Mrs. Dewbrey greeted me solicitously, and her nephew with quiet courtesy, asking if my headache was better.

Somehow I forced myself to join in the conversation, even forced myself to eat something, lest my absence of appetite should cause Mrs. Dewbrey concern. As soon as possible after luncheon, I retired to my room again, but I had not been there long before there was a knock at the door.

'Come in,' I said, and Alice appeared, bearing an envelope on a salver.

I opened it, and read the brief note.

'Dear Miss Meredith' — it ran — 'I know your afternoons are free until tea-time, and I would like to have a talk to you today if possible. If you do not feel well enough, I shall understand. I shall, however, be in the library all afternoon. Alec Dewbrey'.

Despite my weariness, I tidied my hair and went downstairs.

Outside the library I paused and composed myself before knocking. Then I gave a brisk rap, and Mr. Dewbrey bade me enter. He rose and offered me a chair; I sank into its comfortable leather depths, and faced him.

'Miss Meredith, you have had an unhappy experience, you are unwell, and what I have to say is bound to be painful for you,' he began. I said nothing, and he continued.

'I told you some time ago to avoid Hugh Stacey. Unfortunately you ignored what I said, and behaved very foolishly. Thanks to Horatio I was speedily aroused, and out of the house.'

So it was Horatio. I glanced at the dog, lying at Alec Dewbrey's feet.

'Yes — he brought a lady's glove to my room — fortunately, I had not retired. You must have left the kitchen door open — Horatio had the run of the house. He had your scent in his nostrils and we ran straight down to the river. You must have heard him bark — I saw one of the boats was missing . . . '

He broke off. So I had been caught by my own carelessness, leaving the door of the kitchen open, and dropping a glove in my haste.

'So you had really planned to run away with him,' he said quietly.

'Yes. There was no other way.' The tears welled up again. 'We love each other,' I added, in a whisper.

'My dear Miss Meredith, he had no intention of of marrying you. Have you been meeting him at nights, ever since you were forbidden to meet him in the day?'

'Yes,' I said defiantly.

'You have run great risks, then. I must speak to you plainly, there is no other way. Hugh Stacey has recurring attacks of madness — there is tainted blood in him. Not on the Stacey side — rogues a-plenty in that family, but no insanity — no, it's his mother who brought that particular trouble home. It may interest you to learn that she is still alive, Miss Meredith. Alive, but not at large — and neither would young Stacey be if it weren't for Dryden. Have you never wondered why Dryden is such a close companion?'

For the second time within twenty-four hours I felt faint. I sat there, fighting off the dizziness, unable to take my eyes away from Alec Dewbrey's face. It seemed to me that the words he was uttering couldn't possibly be true. I stared unbelievingly into his square-jawed face, but the keen, dark eyes looked unwaveringly back.

'Dryden is his keeper,' he said quietly. 'I gather he warned you off, too.

If you only knew the risks you must have taken! Have you never wondered why the Staceys don't mix — why Hugh Stacey leads such an isolated life?'

'It's not true,' I whispered. 'It's not true — it can't be true!'

'It is true, Miss Meredith.'

'No — no! That man — Dryden . . .'

'A very worthy man indeed. He props up the unfortunate Stacey household. It seems he too got wind there was something going on that night . . . I thank heaven he did. Where did you plan to go?'

'We were going to Scotland to get married.'

I couldn't say any more.

'You really believe he intended to marry you? You poor silly child.'

The look on his face was all too like the look I had seen on Dryden's face in the moonlight.

'There are several very unpleasant things which I could tell you, but which I preferred not to, up to now. Mrs.

Dewbrey had a little dog which disappeared one day, and was found later, floating in the Beck. He had not been drowned; someone had coaxed him across the river and killed him — brutally . . . '

I felt I could bear no more, and attempted to rise, but Alec Dewbrey pushed me gently back.

'You must know these things. You have ignored any warnings given without reasons. You became involved with a tragic young man — tragic, but nonetheless dangerous. The consequences of meeting him secretly could have been grave. You were fortunate that we were able to prevent Hugh Stacey from carrying out his plans. Fortunate, too, I may say, that this business can be hushed up without anyone being the wiser. You will not meet him again — ever. I am certain Dryden will not run any risks in the future.'

My love and my pride lay in ribbons. I sat without speaking, vainly trying to force the tears back. When he spoke again, his voice was gentle.

'I know this has been a shock to you. Please try not to take it too much to heart. Promise you will stay with us — you have made my aunt so happy.'

It seemed to me that all the beauty and romance which had beckoned me had been snatched away, and I had been handed back the familiar companions of duty, obligation, and making others happy. I stood up, and this time he did not prevent me.

'Do not be afraid — I will stay with your aunt,' I said quietly. 'I realise I am useful here, or you would not have gone to such lengths to ensure that I returned here safely. I must thank you for that, Mr. Dewbrey.'

I walked, proud and erect, to the door. Then, suddenly, I could no longer control my outraged pride.

'Whatever you say, Hugh Stacey intended to marry me,' I said, almost choking with emotion. 'He wanted to marry me — he wanted to marry me!'

16

The next few weeks were the saddest and unhappiest of my life. In spite of everything I half expected a letter from Hugh, but no letter came. He and Dryden no longer attended church; only his uncle, upright and remote, took his place in the family pew.

Throughout those long, empty August days, I thought ceaselessly about my lost love. I knew now, with a sad, hopeless knowledge, that Alec Dewbrey had been speaking the truth.

Shut in my bedroom in the afternoons, I spent long hours weeping; thinking about Hugh and myself, and how it had all happened. I remembered the day I had gone to meet him, and he had been missing . . . the mutilated corpse of the squirrel . . . the squirming butterfly impaled on a pin. I remembered too, his occasional moroseness, and his evasiveness about so many things. And I had shut my eyes and trusted him blindly.

I recalled Mr. Dewbrey mentioning the 'Stacey charm' when he was bringing me to Ditchford Hall, after meeting me at the station. Well, Hugh had the charm in full measure; he had everything to attract a young girl. I knew there was no love lost between the Staceys and the Dewbreys, yet Alec Dewbrey's remark about my becoming involved with a 'tragic young man' was not without a certain compassion. And yet, although I accepted much of what Mr. Dewbrey had said, I still did not believe that I had been in danger that night. I believed what I had said — that Hugh had fully intended to take me to Scotland and marry me. I did not know what to do about the necklace he had given me; for the time being at all events there was nothing to do but keep it.

So the days passed. The leaves began

to fall, and the villagers gave thanks for a fine harvest.

My hair was back in ringlets; I held my head high, and attended to Mrs. Dewbrey's every whim. Nevertheless, I mourned for Hugh. I wondered constantly about the state of his mind; I feared he would be worse after the events of that terrible night.

There was nothing I could do; but I could not forget him. Sometimes I thought that Mr. Dewbrey was looking at me with a faintly anxious expression in his eyes. Well, he had no need to fear anything. My tragic, silly, hopeless romance with Hugh Stacey was over.

I could not make up my mind about Mr. Dewbrey and Miss Campion. At one time I had been quite certain that he would not marry her — ever. Now I found I was less certain about many things.

Meanwhile I was not leading an idle life by any means. More and more responsibility was coming my way, as

Mrs. Dewbrey became increasingly inactive.

'Will you see Mrs. Draycott about that, Debbie? Debbie, will you approve of Mrs. Tukes' menu for tonight . . . '

This increased dependence on me did not go unnoticed by her nephew.

'Miss Meredith, my aunt is not very well,' he said one morning. 'Dr. Denton has told me she must rest even more than she is doing, because of her heart condition. I hope you will help in this respect. I think she has realised this herself, though, judging by the number of tasks she entrusts you with.'

'I am glad she does, sir,' I replied. 'As she has such confidence in me, you may be sure I shall not disappoint her.'

'I have no fear of you doing that,' he said gravely. 'I know that we entertain but little at Ditchford Hall these days — nevertheless, I know that my aunt likes everything to be in the best of taste on such occasions. I must congratulate you on the flower arrangement at the dinner table last night.'

In spite of everything, I felt myself flushing with pleasure. During the shortening September days, I looked through the window each morning at a pearl-white mist, which later gave way to sunshine and blue skies. I worked out a time-table for myself, which ensured that I was employed every minute of my waking hours.

'You must take Debbie to hear the Halifield Choral Society sing the *Messiah* at Christmas, Alec,' said Mrs. Dewbrey one day.

Christmas! I was living every day as it came; looking back was painful, looking forward was impossible.

And then the hunting season began, with Penelope Campion much in evidence. Riding superbly, vividly beautiful, she talked much of London, but stayed in Yorkshire. I too rode to hounds, because Mrs. Dewbrey wished me to, and pleasing her was the most important thing in my life now. On her nephew's insistence I was always accompanied by the groom, Ezra Austin.

The clear, bright, autumn days continued. The gardeners swept up the crackling leaves, and the smell of woodsmoke drifted around the gardens. Fires glowed in the rooms at Ditchford Hall; warm shawls were brought out, and people began to talk about Christmas. October turned into November. And one cold, bright, clear day towards the end of the month, we donned hunting pink, and met for the Swalewell Moor Hunt.

The countryside was wintry indeed, now; the ditches were visible, the woods bare-boughed. I was mounted on Aztec, a fine, but quite manageable hunter. Alec Dewbrey told me half jokingly that he would look after me, as the groom had injured his hand, and could not ride. He himself was on Sorrel, who frightened me no less the more I saw of him.

Among the familiar faces at the

Meet, was, of course, the lovely one of Penelope Campion. I knew that however fast and hard the gallop, *she* would be in the foremost ranks, her splendid horse leaping ditch and beck, hedge and drystone wall as they came. Away from the village the hounds soon drew, and we spread out across the undulating countryside of ploughland and grass, moors and woods. The keen air stung my face as Aztec bounded forward, and I felt a slight tremor of nervousness.

I had taken a few jumps on him, but not high ones, and although I had plenty of confidence, I still would have been happier with Ezra Austin in attendance.

The fox had broken covert and was heading for the woods; I saw Sorrel leap ahead, and close behind him, Miss Campion on her fine hunter. The fox was sighted across one of the rides, then part of the pack broke away, having struck the line of a fresh animal, while in the distance I could hear the long sound of the hunting horn.

I was riding fast, but with little sense of direction now. I was usually among the stragglers, but glancing round I realised to my concern that I appeared to be quite alone on an unfamiliar stretch of moorland.

Then, to my great relief I saw a huntsman galloping towards me, and recognised Mr. Dewbrey.

'Where are you going, Miss Meredith?' he called cheerfully. 'You've given me the slip today — you're as elusive as the fox itself! I think we should head *that* way . . .'

He pointed ahead with his riding crop, and just then I noticed two men on horseback galloping from another direction.

They were not huntsmen, and straight away I felt a curious unease.

'Just keep riding,' said Alec Dewbrey brusquely; he kept Sorrel neck and neck with my horse. The other two horsemen bore down on us; they were mounted on a grey horse and Cleveland

Bay respectively, and they carried guns.

Fear and shock seemed to penetrate right into the marrow of my bones — it was Hugh Stacey and Dryden! They were out shooting — we were obviously on Stacey land.

'Keep riding,' repeated Alec Dewbrey.

'Stop! Stop!'

That was Hugh's voice, and instinctively I slowed down Aztec. Mr. Dewbrey moved in closer to me, and I caught sight of Hugh's face, pale, and thinner than I remembered, with his eyes blazing hatred.

'Get off my land, Dewbrey!' he shouted. 'Get off my land!' I could see Dryden was remonstrating with him, but without effect.

'You think you are going to have her, and everything that goes with her — I can see your game, *Squire* Dewbrey! But you won't have her — by God, you won't!'

A shot rang out; I screamed, and both horses reared and whinnied with fright. Aztec leaped forward, nearly unseating me, and Sorrel bolted.

Terrified, I heard the pounding of hooves behind me; another shot rang out; another, and then the sound of a man's voice raised in a dreadful, scarcely human cry; a cry of anguish and betrayal.

Somehow I kept my seat; I wanted to be away from that place at all costs. Far ahead I could see Sorrel, and guessed that he must have the bit between his teeth at last.

I had never ridden on a horse going so fast before, but with a terrible, primitive fear I knew that I must stay on his back, and keep riding, away and off that land. I clung on with all my strength, not daring to look round; ahead, heather and moorland rushed away beneath the hammering of Aztec's hooves, and gave way to green pasture.

A ditch with a hedge behind it rose up before me; I screamed as the horse bunched itself beneath me and leaped over, and yet, I kept my seat.

I could still see the bright speck of Alec Dewbrey's coat in the distance; perhaps he was keeping control of Sorrel after all. My hat had long since gone; my hair came down and streamed around my face; my breath came in gasping sobs.

And then, at last, Aztec began to slow down, and I risked a quick glance behind. There was no one in sight; ahead, fields gave way to woodland.

I had lost sight of Alec Dewbrey behind the trees. I reined Aztec in to a trot, then slowed him up, until finally he stopped in one of the rides. Despite the cold day he was sweating and panting. I drew in a deep breath, and twisted my hair out of the way. I was trembling; I felt sick, and already my arms were aching from my frenzied pulling on the reins.

For a few moments I sat motionless, trying to recover from the shock of seeing Hugh again. Then I urged Aztec along at a steady trot through the woods. There was a numbness inside me; I could scarcely take in the horror of the past few minutes.

Once clear of the woods, though, I knew that worse was to come. In the distance I could see a bright splash of scarlet on the ground. There was no sign of Sorrel; he had unseated Alec Dewbrey despite his superb horsemanship.

I was afraid of what I would find when I reached that still body, even though I made my tired mount quicken his pace.

When at last I reached him and dismounted, icy fear ran though me. Blood was seeping through the sleeve of his coat, a dark, ominous stain on the vivid scarlet cloth. He had been shot by Hugh Stacey!

'Dear God!' I sobbed. His face was ashen, and his eyes closed. I held his wrist, heavy and limp. In spite of his frightening appearance I could feel his pulse beating; he was not dead. He was certainly unconscious though, and in urgent need of a doctor. I stood up and looked desperately around. I could do nothing alone; I must get help, and as quickly as possible. Not from the Staceys' side of the river, though.

There was not a hound nor a huntsman in sight. I mounted Aztec again, and galloped straight ahead. Once before I had been on the Stacey land on horseback, and I had an idea where I was now, from the appearance of the landscape. I judged that Swalewell Beck was not far away.

I could do no more than I was doing, and yet, the awful fear that help would come too late made my breath come in sobs. Any human being would have been welcome, but as I rode desperately, praying for help, the world seemed to be only earth and sky, and bare boughs . . .

No . . . there was another human being, though — the last one I would have thought of. There was a dilapidated cottage, and an old man leaning on the broken gate, almost as if he had been waiting for me.

'Help me!' I cried. 'Please, help me! There's been an accident — there's a gentleman bleeding and unconscious further back there — I'm from the hunt — have they passed this way? I must get help from somewhere!'

I dismounted at the gate. For a moment the old man didn't speak; his rheumy eyes were focussing on me, then, to my horror, he reached out and touched my hair.

'Caldecott!' he exclaimed. 'You're a Caldecott, aren't you? Gerald Stacey put a curse on any Caldecott that came this side o' Swalewell Beck — put a curse on 'em when he was dying . . . You've come back — you're Sarah's bairn, aren't you? I allus knew you'd come back . . . '

'Please!' I cried sharply, my voice cracking like a whip in the winter air — 'I'm from Ditchford Hall, and Mr. Dewbrey is lying where he's been thrown from his horse . . . '

'Aye, from Ditchford Hall,' said the

old man. '*He* used to row down the river to meet her. In service at the Keep, she was . . . '

'Help me!' I cried. 'Has the hunt passed this way? I must get help!'

'The hunt? Nay, they'll never get him now.'

He shook his head. 'He's gone to ground — I heard the horn a while back. He's gone to ground, miss, he's gone to ground. It's the death warning of the Staceys — they call it the Phantom Huntsman. Some say it's all a tale, but I know it's not a tale — I've heard it before — listen! There it goes again!'

He held up his hand triumphantly, and I heard the huntsman's horn, now distant, now close at hand, echoing round and round, as though the river and the trees, and the woodland creatures themselves had taken up the cry:

'Gone to ground! Gone to ground!'

Then, suddenly, it was silent again, with the deep, sleeping silence of the countryside on a November day.

In desperation I mounted Aztec again. Old Wilkins was plainly quite crazy. I would get no help from him, but the hunt couldn't be far away.

I scanned the landscape, and to my tremendous relief I saw two huntsmen cutting across a field lower down.

'Help!' I shouted, as loudly as I could. 'Help! Help!' I turned away from the cottage, and urged Aztec forward again. A minute later a loud shot splintered the still air. Aztec whinnied and reared, with remembered fear. As he wheeled round I saw Wilkins with an ancient blunderbuss pointing upwards.

Again he fired it, and the two huntsmen turned to see me galloping towards them. One of them broke away and rode forward to meet me. After a moment's hesitation the other followed. I felt that my prayers were answered as we drew close enough for recognition. I saw the burly form and rugged features of Farmer Kymes, and hard behind him was Dr. Denton, who did not always follow the hounds.

I thanked God that on this day he had.

17

Ditchford Hall was quiet. Voices were hushed, as the servants went about their duties with sad faces.

Alec Dewbrey lay unconscious in his room, with Horatio a hunched figure crouched down beside the bed. Mrs. Dewbrey was in bed, too, having had a severe heart attack on seeing her nephew carried in, limp and blood-stained. I went from sick room to sick room. All the responsibilities of the household seemed to fall on my shoulders.

Mrs. Draycott, Dan Tulloch, and Stainthorpe the valet, brought their problems to me. Dr. Denton speedily obtained the services of a nurse from Halifield; even so, I got little rest; it was always midnight before I climbed, exhausted, into bed. Day followed day, with no seeming change in Alec

Dewbrey's condition, while his aunt lay, frail and silent in her luxurious bedroom.

I learnt that Hugh Stacey had shot himself, and died shortly afterwards in Dryden's arms. Dr. Denton had been summoned to Swalewell Keep too, but there was nothing to be done there. He told me that it was a clean wound in Alec Dewbrey's arm; the bullet had not touched the bone, but he had lost a lot of blood. It was the blow to his head that was causing the doctor such concern; he was afraid too, that there was a back injury.

After two days he seemed to develop a fever; I heard the doctor and nurse conversing in low tones, and I knew that the situation was grave.

As for Hugh . . . I wept into my pillow; wept for what might have been, thinking of Dr. Denton's gentle words: 'Perhaps, in Hugh Stacey's case, it was all for the best. It's the life of this young man that we must fight for, Miss Meredith.'

'And Mrs. Dewbrey . . . ?' I left the unspoken question in the air.

'She has a worsening heart condition. There are other health troubles, too. We can only try to keep her quiet and resting — she will not walk again, Miss Meredith.'

I turned away to hide my tears.

'Try and be strong, my dear. This is a terrible time for you to be going through, but we need you — Mrs. Dewbrey needs you as never before. You must not fail her.'

And, somehow, I did not fail her. The deeply ingrained teachings of my childhood rose to the surface, and I found a strength I had not known I possessed. I wrote and told my parents of the changed conditions at Ditchford Hall, and received a reply, wise and comforting. They sympathised with me, but pointed out that it was my plain duty to devote all my time to nursing the two patients, and helping the household run smoothly.

Various people from the neighbourhood called to enquire about Mrs.

Dewbrey and her nephew, including Mrs. Campion and Penelope. I felt the hostility from the latter as she saw me busy in the sickrooms, but I no longer cared what she thought.

I knew well enough that although she may be concerned about Mr. Dewbrey's condition, she would not have nursed him and his aunt; would not have sat for hours at bedsides, wiping foreheads and doing the hundred and one duties which comprise sick nursing.

The memory of the day of the hunt haunted me. Why had I gone in that particular direction, and why had Alec Dewbrey followed me? Hugh Stacey's thin, white, face — his eyes blazing with hatred — 'You think you are going to have her, and everything that goes with her!'

What had he meant? Everything that goes with her . . . I looked down at Alec Dewbrey's face, flushed with fever on the lace-trimmed pillow-slip. I was responsible for him being in this condition. If I had obeyed him when he had forbidden me to meet Hugh again, there would have been no talk of eloping, no running away in the night. Hugh would not have been enraged to the point of trying to kill Mr. Dewbrey because he had helped foil his plans to run away with me.

Having ordered the man he hated off his land, Hugh had shot him in his jealousy and madness — and shot to kill. Even though he had failed to do that, Alec Dewbrey lay critically ill as a result of that encounter.

And I was the cause. One man dead . . . the other — no, I could not bear to think about it. I thought of Wilkins, the strange old man in the cottage. He had seemed quite crazy, but he had helped me after all, by firing his blunderbuss into the air to attract attention.

That old man *knew* something about me, but what? Uneasily I recalled the way Tresset the gardener had peered at me when I had first been shown the gardens. Mrs. Tukes, the cook, had stared at me too, and Dan Tulloch had talked about the light playing 'queer tricks'.

During those long, unhappy hours when I sat first at one bedside and then another, Horatio would sometimes crawl along the floor, and put his great head onto my lap, and whine softly. His dreadful, tearless grief distressed me beyond anything.

One afternoon in the midst of all this sadness, Alice, who had been a tower of strength throughout, knocked at the door of Mr. Dewbrey's room, and told me there was a gentleman who wished to see me.

'A Mr. Dryden. He's in the library, miss.'

'Very well, Alice.'

Wearily I made my way to the library; I was tired to the point of exhaustion. As I entered the room, Dryden stood up and bowed. I wished him good day, and asked him to be seated again. He was dressed in mourning. There was an air of restrained sadness about him, and somehow, the old dislike and jealousy which I had felt towards him melted away.

'I shall not take up too much of your time, Miss Meredith. I am here partly on Mr. Stacey's behalf, and partly for my own reasons. Naturally we are concerned about Mr. Dewbrey's condition; Mr. Stacey is deeply grieved, both at his nephew's death, and the fact that he shot Mr. Dewbrey. We have heard that his aunt is ill too.'

'They are both ill. Mr. Dewbrey has a fever — the bullet wound was only in his arm — but that horse threw him . . . '

I broke off, blinking back the tears.

'We found the horse two days after the shooting, Miss Meredith. He had broken a leg, so I did the only thing possible — had him put out of his misery.'

So Sorrel was no more. I had never liked him, but he was Alec Dewbrey's horse, and a very valuable one.

'I believe you gave this to Mr. Hugh,' said Dryden gently, handing me a box which I recognised as being the dressing set which I had bought for his twenty-first birthday. 'I found the card with your birthday message still inside it.'

I took it from him, and broke into uncontrollable sobbing.

'Please don't distress yourself too much. What is past is past. I blame myself for letting him have a gun — but his uncle said he was well enough shooting a few birds with me, and what harm in the boy enjoying himself. Sometimes I could gauge his moods, but sometimes he was unpredictable . . . '

'I didn't know — I didn't know . . . ' I sobbed.

'You didn't know that I had to keep a pretty close watch on him,' said Dryden wearily. 'I took to him years ago, when he was a child, and I was a young man with education and no money. His uncle begged me to take him in my charge, and as he paid me well, and accorded me every privilege, I became committed to him and his nephew. There have been many disadvantages too — we have been very isolated at Swalewell Keep. Sometimes I used to take him to visit his mother — poor lady, she is in a private asylum. That was where we had been when we first met you on the train.'

'He wanted to marry me,' I said, my voice almost a whisper.

For a moment Dryden was silent.

'He enjoyed seeing you in the afternoons. I was never far away, and although I didn't approve wholeheartedly I saw no harm in it at first. Then I became worried. Old Wilkins babbled out some story . . . well, Miss Meredith, I don't wish to pry into your private affairs. This idea of marriage . . . '

He broke off.

'He loved me,' I said. 'He gave me a necklace for an engagement gift — he said it was an heirloom.'

'Then I think you are entitled to keep it. No doubt he took it from his mother's jewellery box — if it was his wish that you should have it, then I think you should. In his way, I believe he was fond of you, but it was not love which made him talk of marriage. However, I do not wish to cause you any more distress. Far be it from me to speak ill of the dead, but Mr. Hugh was very cunning. The way he got out at night to meet you — no, I won't go into that, but it was fortunate indeed that I discovered certain things which aroused my suspicions. Anyway, Swalewell Keep will soon be vacant; I shall accompany old Mr. Stacey abroad. He thinks that is the best plan, and I agree with him.'

'Swalewell Keep vacant?' I exclaimed. 'But who will look after the estate? Will it all be left to the servants?'

'My dear young lady! Surely you know the lease runs out this year?'

'The lease! What lease?'

Dryden looked nonplussed.

'Mr. Hugh never told you the house

and land was all on a lease?'

'I understood it was the Staceys',' I said. 'Why, he shouted at Mr. Dewbrey to get off his land . . . ' I broke off, remembering again the pain of that day.

'He was obsessed with the idea that it should have been his. Old Mr. Stacey accepted the fact that it was leased — and that he would not be able to renew the lease. It was this that Mr. Hugh could not bear.'

'But to whom *does* the land belong?' I asked.

'Why, to Mrs. Dewbrey! It became Caldecott property years ago — one of the Staceys was a compulsive gambler who pledged the whole estate in a game of cards with a Caldecott — and lost! Naturally, it has been the cause of terrible bitterness between the two families.'

For a moment I was speechless with astonishment.

'You never knew until now?' asked Dryden quietly.

'I had no idea. It was never mentioned.'

'I suppose Mrs. Dewbrey is too well bred to flaunt the fact around. And, certainly, Mr. Dewbrey would not mention it. As for Mr. Hugh — well, pride would keep him silent about it. Poor boy, he was the last of the Staceys — the last of the ancient line. A proud family humbled, Miss Meredith. They lost a great deal in the Risings — yes, the Staceys owned every square inch of land for miles around at one time. I never let Mr. Hugh out of my sight after that night you planned to run away. He had all sorts of crazy ideas concerning the house and the land. He would have stopped at nothing to get it back.'

I felt quite dazed.

'Mr. Stacey has enough money to live on comfortably for the rest of his days, but no more than that. In other words, the Staceys are not rich, and Mr. Hugh knew that the lease must run out this year. Moreover, he had very little money on him that night you met him — he had jewellery which I suppose he planned to sell.'

I remembered then how Hugh had reminded me not to forget the necklace. Distasteful though the idea was, I had an unpleasant feeling, that having made me a gift of it, he had intended to sell that too.

'There does seem to be a lot you don't know, Miss Meredith. Were you told the facts about Mr. Hugh?'

'Mr. Dewbrey told me why he had forbidden me to see Hugh after you both stopped us from running away.'

Dryden nodded. 'Mr. Dewbrey is a very fine gentleman. He is above gossiping about his neighbour. I do not know the full story about certain matters, but I should say from my experience of him, Mr. Dewbrey is above a great many things.'

He paused.

'I trust he will recover. If I can be of any service, Miss Meredith . . . '

'Thank you,' I replied, nearly in tears

again. 'We can only hope. I do not leave him for long, except to attend to Mrs. Dewbrey.'

'And how do you find her?'

'She will be an invalid for the rest of her life.'

'Ah . . . I am indeed sorry to hear that.'

He rose, and glanced round the room. 'This beautiful house, Miss Meredith — these rolling acres of land . . . '

Already it was growing dusk, but he walked across to the window, and looked out.

'He was the last of the Staceys,' he repeated softly. 'His uncle would not marry.'

'And the Caldecotts have died out,' I said. 'The end of two great families.'

He turned round, his light grey eyes running over me searchingly.

'With your permission, I will take leave of you now, Miss Meredith. And I hope to hear better news before long.'

After some hesitation, he told me

that Hugh's grave was in the new part of the churchyard, the family vault having been blocked up.

'It is very open where he is. The wind blows straight across from the moors. He would have liked that — it's so free and wild.'

'Thank you for telling me — I know what you mean,' I said. 'And thank you for coming, Mr. Dryden.'

Rather shyly I held out my hand, and his strong clasp made me realise how alone I was in that great house, and how I longed to hear Alec Dewbrey's masculine voice about the place again.

* * *

And, to my great joy, within a few days I did hear it. Very weak, it is true, but he spoke one morning, and asked what day it was.

'You have been ill for a long time,' I said. 'Please do not excite yourself, Mr. Dewbrey. Dr. Denton will be here shortly.'

When he did arrive, I greeted him with a smile — the first for a long time.

'He is still very weak,' said the good doctor, after he had seen the patient. 'That is natural, of course. But things are very much better, Miss Meredith. We have a great deal to be thankful for.'

'A great deal,' I agreed. 'I will take you to Mrs. Dewbrey now.'

The doctor paused for a moment outside her room.

'Concerning Mrs. Dewbrey — while her nephew was still in danger I did not wish to upset you more than necessary, but she is in a very poor way. There are complications, and she will grow weaker. I must warn you, you have a hard time ahead.'

For the time being, Mrs. Dewbrey appeared to have lost interest in everything. Sometimes she gave me a vague, sweet smile, but most of the time she lay back on the pillows, staring in front of her.

Christmas came and went, with little festivity at Ditchford Hall. Naturally, there was no entertaining. I had heard that the Mummers from the village always called to give their show on Christmas Eve, but this year they did not call, there being so much sickness in the house. On Christmas Eve I sat crocheting a cobweb-fine shawl for Mrs. Dewbrey, thinking how her nephew had not been able to take me to hear the Halifield Choral Society sing the *Messiah* after all.

However, I exchanged Christmas greetings with him; he was now propped up in bed, and growing stronger every day.

I did not tell him of Dryden's visit, nor of Sorrel's fate; still less of Hugh Stacey's. He would have to know, but not yet. I told him his aunt was unwell, as, perforce, I was bound to. I gave a great deal of thought to my conversation with Dryden. My dislike of him had really been based on the fact that he had frequently made a third party when I had wanted to be alone with Hugh. He had had a difficult duty to perform; if he had failed to protect Hugh from himself in the end, he had no cause for self-reproach.

I had thought Alec Dewbrey so wrong in his attitude, and he had been so right. I understood, too, Hugh's bitter words about Dewbrey acting the squire; aware of his tainted blood, humiliated by his position, the last of the Staceys feared that a man who 'was not even a Caldecott' would one day inherit Swalewell Keep.

But why had he planned to marry me? For in spite of everything, I still felt sure he had.

There were so many problems, and so many things to think about. But the important thing at the moment was to nurse Alec Dewbrey back to health, and do what I could for his aunt.

As Mr. Dewbrey's condition improved, Penelope Campion began to visit more often, despite the bad weather. Sometimes she would come with her mother, and pay a duty visit to Mrs Dewbrey before proceeding to Alec's room. On these occasions she was soon followed by Mrs. Campion.

There were times, though, when she would drive over alone, often bringing some delicacy for the two patients. At such times she would remain with Mr. Dewbrey for an hour or more.

He will never marry her, I thought, sitting at Mrs. Dewbrey's bedside. But suppose he did? I thought of her slender white hand, with a half-hoop of diamonds glittering on the third finger.

She had not spent the winter months nursing two sick people — she looked fresh and radiant in her brown velvet costume with a fur cape over her shoulders, and a matching fur hat, tilted forward in the latest style.

I looked tired and drawn. But why was I comparing myself with her?

'You have been wonderful during this trying time,' she remarked once, as she was leaving. 'I do appreciate what you have done for Mr. Dewbrey. Mama was saying what a blessing it was that his aunt engaged your services as a companion.'

'How kind of you, Miss Campion,' I said. Inwardly I was enraged at her patronising manner. *She* appreciated what I had done for him!

Something almost like physical pain seemed to twist inside me. I thought of those long, terrible days when I had sat with Horatio, and vowed that if Alec Dewbrey recovered, I would ask nothing more from life. But what was I asking from life now?

'Miss Meredith, your duties as a sick nurse are at an end as far as I am concerned,' he told me rather abruptly, the following day. 'You have been doing far too much, and it is quite unnecessary now. I shall be leaving my room next week, and resuming normal life as soon as possible. I know that I owe you a great deal . . . '

'You owe me nothing, sir,' I said.

'I am the best judge of that. I know that my aunt is ill; I hope to see her tomorrow. And the doctor has told me what is wrong with her.'

I wondered what else the doctor had told him, but I was not left wondering for long.

'He told me about the tragedy over at Swalewell Keep, too.'

For a moment I turned away, unable to face him. To my surprise, I felt his hand on my shoulder, comforting and protective.

'My dear Miss Meredith, I am sorry that you have been caused such pain . . . '

He broke off.

'Sorrel is dead, too,' I said. It was a stupid sort of remark to make, clumsy and ill-timed.

'I know. I would not have lost control of him if I had not been wounded in the arm — but it is not important now.'

'No,' I said. 'Misty is growing up, anyway.'

'Misty is yours as soon as he is old enough.'

Alec Dewbrey spoke decisively. Evidently he took it for granted I would still be there when Misty was ready for a rider.

Anyway, why were we talking about horses? Surely Sorrel's death was the least important thing which had happened.

'I have brought a lot of trouble to Ditchford Hall,' I said, trying to keep my voice steady.

'One could as easily say Ditchford Hall had brought a lot of trouble to you. Don't blame yourself for a set of circumstances which were not of your making.'

He seemed about to say more on the same lines, but when he spoke again it was merely to observe that Horatio had grown far too fat sitting around the bedroom.

'He only goes out of the house for a few minutes at a time. He needs proper exercise — perhaps you will walk with him in the grounds when the weather permits, now that you are no longer tied to two sickrooms. I hope to be out and about myself before long, but meanwhile I am sure some fresh air will be beneficial to you as well as Horatio.'

'I have no doubt it will, sir,' I said, and left the room, to see how Mrs. Dewbrey was. She too seemed improved, and I told her that her nephew was much better, and would be coming to see her.

That night I sat in my nightgown and wrapper in front of the fire in my room. I had stopped keeping my diary during the time of Alec Dewbrey's illness, being far too busy with other matters. Now, however, I took it out, and made the prosaic entry that he no longer needed me.

He no longer needed me . . . he no longer needed me . . . except perhaps to exercise Horatio. Tomorrow, no doubt Penelope Campion would visit again; conditions were ideal; he was inactive and housebound.

Since I had arrived at Ditchford Hall, Alec Dewbrey had ridden with me, played the piano with me; danced with me. He had talked to me about his aunt's health; he had discussed the business of running the estate, he had complimented me on my toffee making.

He had told me my ball gown was too low; he had forbidden me to see Hugh Stacey, and when I had defied him, he had rushed out into the night to prevent me from running away with him. He had been shot at on my account, he had been injured, and had been gravely ill.

I knew now with a sad knowledge that my wayward and foolish heart must be carefully controlled.

What I had felt for Hugh had been infatuation; I realised that now. But more than that, I realised that I was in love with Alec Dewbrey, truly in love.

And he no longer needed me . . .

18

Once Mr. Dewbrey was up and about again, he seemed to gain strength rapidly. I mentioned to him that Dryden had visited the house during the time of his illness, and told me that he and old Mr. Stacey were to live on the continent.

Mr. Dewbrey nodded.

'Yes, Swalewell Keep will soon be empty.'

'I wonder what will happen to that old man in the cottage by the river,' I mused. 'He fired a blunderbuss into the air that day, and attracted the attention of Farmer Kymes and Dr. Denton.'

'There is no reason why he should not stay there for the rest of his life — I shall make sure he is not in any want. I suppose you were not aware that the Staceys were tenants of my aunt's?'

'Not until Mr. Dryden told me.'

He seemed about to say more, but changed his mind, thinking, no doubt, that anything connected with the Staceys was painful for me to discuss.

'You still have headaches, sir,' I observed, seeing him pass his hand uneasily over his forehead.

'Sometimes. Dr. Denton says they will go eventually. The main thing is that I will have no lasting health troubles following my accident — a few backaches and headaches for a while, perhaps. I believe in some cases illness can have its uses — it can make one realise the important things in life.'

He looked at me very hard when he said this, as though the remark had some particular significance.

'If you will excuse me, I must see if Mrs. Dewbrey is awake,' I said, feeling uncomfortable under his steady gaze.

'I expect to be very busy dealing with the Swalewell Keep estate for the next few weeks,' he said. 'Give as much time as you can to my aunt, but do not neglect your own health.'

We were in the library, his favourite room, and one which I was growing increasingly fond of. He stood up when I did, and reaching forward, clasped my hands.

I was taken by surprise; tingles of delight ran through me at the warm contact, although it only lasted seconds.

He released my hands, and opened the door for me. I left the room feeling baffled, and went to see Mrs. Dewbrey.

She was propped up on the pillows, a muslin cap on her head, and the shawl I had crocheted over her shoulders. She had spoken more during the past week; although frail, she looked much better. She did not know the details of her nephew's accident, and certainly, nobody would be likely to tell her them. She thought Sorrel had bolted and thrown Alec, something which she had always feared.

'Debbie, I would like you to make arrangements for my solicitor to come from Halifield and see me as soon as possible,' she said. 'Alec will give you the details about him. Write and say I wish to see him concerning a matter of importance.'

'Very well, ma'am,' I said, adding that she was looking better.

She gave a rather sad smile. 'I have this curious stiffness down one side — my left arm and hand don't feel as they should. However, while I am as well as this, I will attend to some of my affairs.'

When I asked Mr. Dewbrey for particulars of his aunt's solicitor, he looked rather thoughtful, but supplied the necessary information.

I wrote to the gentleman, and a few days later he came to see his client. He was a tall, scholarly looking man, a Mr. Smailes, and he brought his partner, Mr. Turnbull, with him.

I took them to Mrs. Dewbrey's room, and rather to my surprise Dr. Denton arrived shortly after them. I explained that she had two solicitors with her, but he did not appear surprised; he said she was expecting him, too. Normally he always called on alternate mornings now Mr. Dewbrey was convalescent. However, he was shown to her room, and I retreated to my own, to write some letters.

I decided that if the gentlemen were still with Mrs. Dewbrey I had better send Alice up to see if afternoon tea was to be served in the room.

She came back with word that the doctor was leaving, as he had other calls to make, but that the solicitors were having tea with Mrs. Dewbrey, and would I join them in her room.

I hastened to do so, and found her looking tired, but happy and relaxed. Mr. Smailes and Mr. Turnbull were surprisingly cheerful and pleasant men once they dropped their soberly professional expressions.

I poured out the tea, and we talked about general matters until the gentlemen took their leave.

Afterwards Mrs. Dewbrey told me that she had cleared up a number of matters to her satisfaction.

That evening I was going downstairs, just as Alec Dewbrey was about to ascend.

I had dined with his aunt in her room, and I guessed he would be going to see her.

Horatio rushed upstairs somewhat clumsily, and in his exuberance he pushed against me and caused me to miss my footing. With a cry I pitched forward, and would have fallen down the last few steps had his master not rushed up them and caught me.

'Are you all right — my dearest — Miss Meredith?'

I was shaken but unhurt, thanks to his swift action. But I was in his arms, and he had called me 'my dearest'! The Miss Meredith had been tacked on afterwards.

'Yes — thank you . . . ' I said, somewhat breathlessly. He did not release me, though. Instead, he kissed me a long, lingering kiss that threw me into a wild tumult of emotion.

The strength of his arms around me,

the hardness of his lips coming down on mine took me completely by surprise. And yet, I knew that this was what I had been waiting for . . .

19

For the first time in many months I knew the meaning of happiness again. The morning after he had broken my fall I lay awake in bed, thinking of Alec Dewbrey. I remembered the way I had responded to his kisses; the way I had felt in his arms; secure, protected, as I had never felt in poor Hugh's.

'Can you forget Hugh Stacey?' he had asked, still holding me. 'You are so young, Debbie — so vulnerable. You have faced so many situations since you first came here. Sometimes we cannot understand our own hearts until there is a crisis of some sort. I thought it was not possible that a girl of eighteen could make such a difference to my life. I was quite pleased when Aunt Caroline said she was getting a companion. She asked me to go to Halifield to meet you, and from the moment I first set eyes on you — I can't explain how I felt. I was angry with myself because I cared — I cared so desperately about you . . . '

He broke off and embraced me again.

'When I was very young, I fell deeply in love with someone. She was pretty and shallow — a butterfly, nothing more — but at the time I was too infatuated to see that. She hurt me deeply; after that experience, I vowed I would not lose my heart again in a hurry. The years pass swiftly, but wounds as deep as that take a long time to heal. I may strike you as being detached and unfeeling, or perhaps somewhat staid and set in my ways — I am not really. When someone has suffered as I did, it is not unusual for them to be on the defensive.'

Now I understood the things about him which had formerly baffled me. I had always felt that he avoided any tying relationship with a woman; that even Penelope Campion with all her charm and beauty would not lure him into a proposal.

He was trembling as he held me in his arms, and for a few moments I felt wild delight and triumph. He was not a man to kiss lightly — he was not a man to wear his heart on his sleeve!

'What about Miss Campion?' I asked, rather surprised at my own boldness.

'Mrs. Campion is a friend of my aunt's — it would be discourteous not to be pleasant to her daughter.'

'She is in love with you,' I said.

'Whatever her feelings towards me, I have never trifled with her affections — or, indeed, those of any woman. Surely only *my* feelings count, Debbie. At my age, a man is capable of conducting his life with discretion. For the time being, all I ask from you is that you can give me some hope for the future — that you can put the past behind you.'

For the next few days Alec's manner towards me was gravely correct in front of the servants; only when we were alone did he reveal his feelings, and then, always with restraint.

He was extremely busy; old Mr. Stacey had left for the continent with Dryden, and there was much to do at Swalewell Keep. I was busy caring for Mrs. Dewbrey, and in the afternoons, when I was sometimes free, Alec was invariably out, occupied either with Ditchford Hall estate, or Swalewell Keep.

A few kisses in the library; a swift embrace in the breakfast-room each morning — this was all the display of affection for the time being, and yet, it was enough.

Spring was slowly, feebly, breaking through, and when I looked in the mirror now, my eyes glowed with a soft radiance, and I felt a woman, as I had never felt before.

Mrs. Dewbrey was still confined to her room, and one afternoon, having settled her comfortably for a nap, I sat embroidering in her sitting-room.

I had not been there long before Crowther, the butler, announced Miss Campion's arrival.

'Show her in here,' I said, and a few moments later Penelope Campion appeared She was wearing a light blue walking costume, trimmed with navy blue braid, and looked particularly stylish and distinguished. I felt no envy, though. Perhaps for the first time I felt as though I were meeting her on equal terms — indeed, on terms that were more than equal.

Miss Campion explained that her mother had a bad headache, but that she had come over to pay her respects to Mrs. Dewbrey.

'I am afraid she is asleep at the moment,' I said.

'And — er — Mr. Dewbrey?'

'He is busy attending to affairs at Swalewell Keep.'

'Is he indeed?'

The blue eyes snapped; the patronising manner which Penelope Campion always adopted towards me vanished abruptly. She eyed me with open hostility.

'Quite the fine lady now, aren't you — Miss what-is-it? Meredith? Oh, yes, my girl, I've heard stories about you — no better than your mother, by all accounts.'

'My mother?' I gasped, and had a sudden, swift vision of my gentle, blameless parent.

'Yes, your mother — a parlour maid, nothing more. You're a by-blow — and that poor, silly old lady lying in her room thinks you're her son's by-blow at that! She thinks *he's* your father!'

She waved her hand contemptuously at the portrait of Will Caldecott, the son whose name was never mentioned in that house.

'Old servants remember things, and gossip. You think men can't resist you — men far above your station in life. You set your cap at poor crazy Hugh Stacey — oh, yes, I know. And now, if you please, you have the audacity to set it at Alec Dewbrey. You contemptible little slut!'

For a moment I felt frozen with horror and disbelief.

It was unbelievable that a lovely and gracious girl like Penelope Campion could descend to this level; utter these deadly insults with such venom.

'Do you imagine a gentleman like Mr. Dewbrey would want *you* — except as men wanted your mother? As you sit here embroidering no doubt you see yourself as *Mrs*. Dewbrey, the fine lady, one day. The Dewbreys are a very good family — do you think he would be likely to marry a nothing — a love child? There is only one reason why a man of birth and breeding would marry you — and Alec Dewbrey would never stoop to that. Never!'

She paused for breath.

I fought against the faintness I was beginning to feel; the shock of what she had said seemed to stun me. Nevertheless, I drew myself up, and looked at her with scorn.

'*I* could never stoop as low as you have stooped this afternoon,' I said levelly. 'You have repeated servants' gossip, called me foul names, and thrown doubts on my parentage. One thing is certain, and you know it to be certain, that is why you are so angry. Whatever his feelings towards me, Mr. Dewbrey will never marry *you* — never! He is much too wise for that.'

She went white. She was beyond speech; I had put into words what I suspected she knew in her heart. Without saying anything further she turned and left the room, and, presumably, the house.

Only after she had gone did the full impact of her words really strike home. I looked at the portrait over the mantelpiece. Was it my imagination, or was there something familiar in the arch of the brow; in the curve of the mouth?

A by-blow — a love child? I thought of my parents, and the way I had been sent to Mrs. Dewbrey, and told by Papa to give it a twelvemonth. I thought of the way I had been treated at Ditchford Hall, more like a daughter than a companion.

Was I being gossiped about in the village? A by-blow; a love child . . . but if there was any truth in what Miss Campion had said — a Caldecott!

Suddenly I thought of old Wilkins down by the river. I had tried to put him out of my mind, but now I knew that I must visit him. If he knew anything about me, I wanted to hear what it was. Naturally, despite the shocked state I was in, I longed to tell Alec what Penelope Campion had said, but I knew that I could never do that.

Ever since I had come to Ditchford Hall ill luck had dogged my happiness. I had misjudged people, I had made mistakes, and somehow, everything had gone wrong. There had been something mysterious about my coming to the place right from the start. Time after time I had been puzzled by things; by curious looks, half-heard conversations;

things hinted at. But I could never, never be what Penelope Campion had called me!

Somehow the afternoon passed, but needless to say, I did not pick up my embroidery again.

I paced the room restlessly, unable to think of anything except what Penelope Campion had said. Well, she had certainly come out into the open, and shown her jealous heart to me.

I walked over to the window, and looked out. It was a dry, windy day. If it was no worse tomorrow, I would have Pansy saddled, ride into the village, and go onto the Swalewell Keep side of the river. Old Wilkins always seemed to be at home — although I supposed that sometimes he must go into the village. If he sought companionship there, he may well have talked about the shooting; about other things, too.

At tea time I went to Mrs. Dewbrey's room, and found her in a rather strange mood.

'Please help me into the chair,

Debbie,' she said.

'If you feel well enough, ma'am.'

I spoke doubtfully. She did not look very well to me. However, she was insistent that I should help her into the chair, which I did, rather nervously. I noticed her frail hands trembling as she sipped her tea which I gave her. She ate nothing; neither did I. I was too upset at what had taken place that afternoon, and apart from that I was filled with unbearable sadness at the deterioration in her condition.

'Is Alec in?'

'No, ma'am, not yet. I expect he will visit you later in the evening.'

'I feel so tired, Debbie.'

The tears began to gather in my eyes. In spite of the sickness in the house, I had experienced a few wonderful days of happiness because I knew that Alec Dewbrey cared for me.

Now my happiness was shattered again. Penelope Campion's visit and Mrs. Dewbrey's condition combined to bring my spirits as low as possible. I stayed with her, and dined with her later, but the food was sent back practically untasted. For the most part we sat in silence; I did not offer to read to her, and she did not ask me to.

I had an intense longing to ask her about her son; to get her to drop the proud face which she presented to the world, and to tell me what really happened. I could not believe that what Penelope Campion said was true, and yet . . .

Later, Alec came in, and we sat talking quietly. I saw the affection and concern in his eyes when he looked at his aunt; I saw love in them when he looked at me. He had respect for me too; let Miss Campion say what she may, he did not regard me as she had suggested. Nevertheless, I was too upset to respond to his conversation with more than a few brief words, and a smile.

After about an hour he said he was going into the library. I said I would stay with his aunt, and make her comfortable for bed. I knew that he hoped I would see him later in the evening. When I helped Mrs. Dewbrey back into bed, she seemed in a very emotional state.

'Debbie! My child,' she said, and slipped her wasted arms around me. 'Kiss me.'

I did so, and having prepared her for the night, I left the room quietly, and went to my own.

If Alec hoped I would go into the library, he would be disappointed. I felt I could not behave naturally, could not let him kiss me, after what I had been told that afternoon.

20

I reined in Pansy, and took a deep breath. In front of me stood Wilkins' tumbledown cottage, with torn, dirty curtains hanging at the windows. What I was about to do required courage.

I dismounted, walked up the garden path, and stood in front of the door, with its peeling wood, and large iron knocker. I gave a loud rat-tat-tat! on the door. In any case, I told myself, whether I got any satisfaction or not from this visit, it was only an act of normal kindness to see how the old man was faring now the Staceys had gone.

There was no response from within, and I knocked again. This time there were movements from inside; dragging footsteps, and the door was opened, just wide enough to let the occupant see who was knocking. I repressed a feeling of distaste; how ill and neglected the old man looked.

'Good day,' I said briskly. 'I thought I would call and see how you were . . . '

He recognised me.

'You've come,' he said, and opened the door wide. 'I've been badly all t' winter. Come in.'

I followed him in uneasily.

'I used to look after the game,' he said vaguely. 'Used ter do all sorts.'

The outer door opened straight into the house. It was depressingly poor, dirty and neglected. There was a rough deal table, two wooden chairs, and a horsehair sofa and chair, both in a state of dilapidation.

'Sit down,' he said, indicating the chair.

He had an attack of coughing, and I sat, embarrassed and ill at ease, half wondering if it had been a good idea to come after all. There was a log fire burning in the hearth, and on the dirty chimney-piece a framed pencil sketch of a girl.

I looked at it, and his eyes followed

mine. He took it off the nail, and handed it to me.

'You know who it is,' he said.

I looked at the delicate features sketched lightly in; the wide cheekbones and pointed chin; the slanting eyes. A signature was scribbled in the corner — W. A. Caldecott.

'Your mother,' he said simply. '*He* drew her. Used to row downt' river to see her. No, he couldn't leave her alone — we threw her out int' finish. Maisie didn't want to, but I'd had enough — she were having a baby. Nay, lass, I wish I hadn't now — after Maisie died it were nowt in this house. But I turned her out, and she'd nowhere to go — we heard she'd gone crying to the curate, and they'd tekken her in, and she'd had it and died! A little girl, and the curate up and moved away! Mrs. Caldecott at Ditchford Hall would have nowt to do with it; young Caldecott had been missing for a few months — aye — he cleared off and left her! Next thing we heard he'd died of a fever or summat abroad, and that were the end of the Caldecotts.'

He paused, looking at me.

'Nay,' he said softly. 'Not quite the end of the Caldecotts. She sent for you, didn't she, after all these years? I knew who you were soon as I saw you. You're like him, but you're like her, too. Little Sarah Bailey. She was your mother, and when she came from the orphanage to work at Swalewell Keep, Maisie and me took to her.'

He broke off to cough again.

'She lived with us here,' he went on, 'And worked at Keep. Aye — and now Swalewell Keep's empty, and young Mr. Hugh dead, and old Mr. Stacey off abroad wi' Mr. Dryden.'

He shook his head, and his eyes were sad.

'I telled Mr. Hugh you were a Caldecott. Caldecotts should stay the other side ot' Beck — the curse falls on any that come this side — nay, it's true, lass — there's no good'll come to you ont' Stacey side!'

He rambled on, like any old man who lived alone, and regretted the past. But I knew that what he had told me was the truth.

I looked round the miserable, neglected room. My mother had lived there, but I had no doubt that in those days the cottage had been a place with a certain homely comfort.

'Maisie was twenty years younger than me, and she went first,' he said. 'Never had any children of our own. But when Sarah come, she was fourteen, and she lived with us for seven years. He were always up and down the Beck looking for her — I coulda drowned him. He shoulda stuck to his own sort — not that Sarah weren't beautiful — she were as good in her blue gown as owt that ever passed through Ditchford Hall gates.'

So I was what Penelope Campion had called me — a love child, a by-blow. Through a blur of tears I looked down at the drawing in my hand.

'I'm sorry I turned your mother out, lass,' said the old man gruffly. 'Looks as if the lady at the Hall is sorry for what she did, too. I was hard — but mind you — I wasn't any harder than she was — and young Will Caldecott was her own flesh and blood. You're her flesh and blood, too, think on.'

He coughed again. 'Is she good to you — the old lady?'

'She is kind and good,' I said. 'But she is ill.'

'Ah! Ill, is she? Yes, I heard they had trouble at Hall. And Mr. Dewbrey — they say he got better.'

'He is well now. He will be coming to see you. You did help that day, firing your gun.'

He smiled. 'It wer nowt. Always have it handy . . . tell me, was t' curate and his wife good to you?'

'The most wonderful parents,' I said quietly. 'Whatever happened between my mother and Will Caldecott, I think of my father and mother as being the people who brought me up. I had no reason to believe I was not their daughter until recently. Believe me, I have no regrets that you turned my mother out, and that she went to the curate and his wife.'

'Then I'm glad, lass, for your sake. They med a lady on you, and we could never ha' done that. Perhaps it were all for the best — Sarah woulda died anyhow, and Maisie went sudden, so I woulda bin left with you. And I couldn't have done much for you.'

He looked relieved.

'We were fond of her, you know,' he went on, and I knew that whatever I said, he would always reproach himself for turning out the girl who had shared their home and had their love for seven years.

I asked him if he was in need of anything, but he said not.

Apparently he had been given a small annuity by the Staceys; enough, seemingly, to keep him. He added that he would be better when the warm weather came. I stood up, ready to go.

''Appen the old lady will see thee all right,' he said, shuffling to the door behind me.

He stood and watched me untie Pansy's reins.

'Good-bye,' I said, and with a wave to him, I urged the horse into a trot. I wanted to get away from that cottage with its ghostly memories. In spite of keeping outwardly calm, I was deeply shocked at what he had told me. A whole host of bits and pieces began to fit themselves together.

People remembered things, old rumours were dug up; servants tittle-tattled below stairs. I thought of Hugh, and his plans to marry me. I understood now what had baffled me before. The bitter truth was that Hugh had only talked of marriage after Wilkins had revealed my identity to him. On that ride back to Ditchford Hall, I saw with terrible clarity exactly what Dryden had meant that day when he had called to see me.

' . . . He had all sorts of ideas concerning the house and land. He would have stopped at nothing to get it back . . . '

Hugh had questioned me very carefully about my position at Ditchford Hall, and how I was treated there. I had been right about his intentions to marry me. Yes, he had meant to do that, but only because he hoped that as Mrs. Dewbrey's grandchild I would surely inherit the estate.

I reflected grimly that failing that, he would have had the satisfaction of knowing that he had wreaked a terrible revenge on Mrs. Dewbrey and her nephew.

I thought of Alec Dewbrey; his restraint; his attempts to keep me away from Hugh without revealing the unpleasant facts, until finally, he had to.

Penelope Campion's ugly words came back to me 'The Dewbrey's are a very good family — do you think he would be likely to marry a nothing — a love child?'

Yet Hugh Stacey had been prepared to do just that, for his own ends. But then Hugh had not been a normal man.

Of all the things which had happened to me since I had set foot in Ditchford Hall, learning of my true parentage was the bitterest.

It turned my whole world upside down, and made me see people in a different way altogether. It began to drizzle, but I scarcely noticed it, I was so busy with my thoughts.

I turned Pansy into the drive, and galloped her through what had now become heavy rain.

At the stables, John Stubbs met me with an anxious face.

'Miss Meredith — the whole house has been looking for you — they didn't think to come to the stables for a bit — we didn't know where you were. It's the mistress — she's been tekken very ill.'

He helped me dismount. I was quite past speaking. I swept my damp habit over my arm, and hurried into the house through the back way.

21

For the next few days I seemed to be living in a dream. Alec and I spent hours at Mrs. Dewbrey's bedside, with Horatio crouching at our feet. People came and went softly; Dr. Denton joined us in our vigil from time to time. Everywhere voices were hushed; the whole house seemed as if waiting for the end.

Then, early one morning, Mrs. Dewbrey recovered consciousness, and recognised us both. She smiled faintly at Alec, and then turned towards me. Her hands moved restlessly, as if she was trying to tell me something. I reached forward, and clasped them both in mine.

I sat like that for a long time; I was surprised when Alec gently lifted my hands away.

'It is all over, Debbie,' he said.

Horatio stood up and gave a long, miserable howl. Ditchford Hall was without a mistress, and, I told myself, as I tumbled, dazed and shocked into my bed, I was without an employer.

Alec had insisted on my going to bed, even though it was nearly six o'clock in the morning.

The shock of finding Mrs. Dewbrey so ill when I returned from Wilkins' cottage had driven away my preoccupation with my parentage. I sank into bed, overwhelmed with sorrow and weariness. Nature took over, and after some restless tossing around, I fell asleep, and slept until late afternoon.

Once I was up again, there were so many things to see to, even though Alec had been busy all day. There were letters to write, people to see, and, of course, mourning to be ordered. Throughout all this, Alec was the essence of kindness and thoughtfulness.

How much did he know about me — if anything? Penelope Campion and her mother had called at the house, but

I made a point of not seeing them.

There was an atmosphere of both sadness and repressed excitement evident below stairs. I supposed this was because many of the servants had been with Mrs. Dewbrey for years, and the reading of the will was imminent. I hastened from task to task in my hurriedly made mourning gown.

I had written home and told my parents about her death. Needless to say, I had not mentioned the story I had heard from Jonas Wilkins. I was in a state of tension about everything, and I wanted the funeral to be over and the will to be read, before I approached my parents.

Mama had replied to my letter, saying that she and Papa were sure that I had done my duty towards Mrs. Dewbrey.

'We are so very proud of you, Debbie . . . ' ran the letter. 'To leave home as you did, at eighteen, and to deal with so many problems, with sickness and death, cannot have been easy. We are longing to see you before long, but do not rush away. There may yet be work for you to do at Ditchford Hall . . . '

It was the day before the funeral, and I stood in the drawing-room with the letter in my hand. Something about that letter from home made the tears gather in my eyes.

The door opened, and Alec came in. He looked distinguished in his black suit, but his face was pale and drawn.

'Debbie!' he said, and slipped his arms around me. 'Don't cry, dearest. The stress and strain of all this will be over tomorrow. Is it a letter from your parents?'

'Yes,' I whispered, after a long hesitation. I wanted so to say: 'They're not my parents, Alec. I'm just a foundling — a love child of the Caldecotts.'

But somehow, the words wouldn't come. And I wanted so to be held in his arms, to feel the comfort of his body close to mine.

'Debbie, I do so want to see you happy. I was very fond of my aunt, and she was of me. I never knew anything but goodness and kindness from her. She lost her own son years ago — did she ever tell you?'

'No,' I said, my voice muffled on his shoulder. 'I heard about it from the housekeeper. If she had lived, I believe she would have told me about it in time, though. I think she wanted to.'

Standing there with Alec's arms around me, I had the fleeting illusion of happiness, but I knew that it was only an illusion.

'She was very fond of you, too, Debbie,' he went on. 'She made a new will that day when she saw her solicitors. She told me about it, and said she had tried to be absolutely fair both to me — and to you, Debbie.'

I remained silent.

'She also told me that she did not think she had much longer to live. She said that after her death she hoped I would behave in a fitting manner towards you. I was unable to understand that remark, but she merely smiled and said I would understand at the time.'

'Your aunt could be very secretive,' I said, and gently disengaged myself. I was trembling inwardly, wondering what tomorrow would bring.

We did not continue our conversation, as the butler announced that Mr. and Mrs. Sheard had called.

The next day I rose early, and dressed with the assistance of Alice. An atmosphere of strain and sadness pervaded the whole house, and to make things worse the weather was appalling; wind driven rain lashed against the windows. I reflected that we would all be soaked and frozen before Mrs. Dewbrey was laid to rest. Despite the terrible day, though, everything went as planned; the long, slow drive to Swalewell church; the black horses with their bobbing plumes, the vicar intoning the burial service, and Alec dropping a fragment of moist earth onto his aunt's coffin.

I had been secretly to visit Hugh's grave; it was not far away from Mrs. Dewbrey's. I was thankful for the heavy veil which hid my face from the world. In spite of the inclement weather, all the village had turned out to pay their last respects to the gracious lady who had been the Mistress of Ditchford Hall for so many years.

I felt the touch of Alec's hand under my arm, comforting and reassuring . . . somehow, the funeral was over, and the will was being read.

I saw Mr. Smailes eyeing me rather nervously. He glanced round the rose drawing-room at the assembled company, and coughed.

' . . . the last will and testament . . . Caroline Elizabeth Dewbrey . . . ' His voice was expressionless as he proceeded to read it. I sat shivering, knowing that I would be mentioned, and yet not knowing what to expect. I knew that there were others in the room; I knew that Alec was in the room, and yet I felt curiously alone.

'. . . To my grand-daughter, Deborah Meredith, as she is known, the daughter of my late son, William Arthur Caldecott, I bequeath Ditchford Hall . . . the entire estate . . . '

I sat without moving, quite dazed as the voice droned on, revealing all the details of my position. Mr. Smailes and his partner were my trustees up to the age of twenty-one, or in the event of my marriage.

'. . . To Alexander Richard Dewbrey . . . nephew . . . Swalewell Keep . . . '

A gasp seemed to rise in the room; I felt a sickly faintness steal over me. Even though I already knew the facts it was a shock to realise it was no secret from anyone now; my position had been made plain to all. My mother, poor, pretty little Sarah Bailey had not even been mentioned. I sat there, wealthy, but illegitimate; my relationship to Mrs. Dewbrey dramatically revealed. Mr. Smailes' voice went on, but it seemed to be coming from a long way off. There was a lengthy list of bequests to servants; no one had been forgotten.

Afterwards he tried to explain to me certain matters connected with my inheritance. I was still too overwhelmed to understand very much about it; he seemed to realise that, and simplified matters by telling me in slightly admonishing tones that I was a very rich young lady indeed.

'What about Mr. Dewbrey?' I asked hesitantly.

'Well, as you heard, he's got Swalewell Keep, and the land. No additional money, but then I have no doubt he has means of his own. Mrs. Dewbrey's will merely bears out the old saying that blood is thicker than water.'

Blood is thicker than water . . . I wanted to see Alec, but he was nowhere in evidence; I supposed he was busy as usual, so I went to my room, and closed the door.

This great house and the servants in it were mine; money, land, jewellery and possessions were all mine. I had inherited the 'rolling acres' which Dryden had talked about.

I threw myself on the bed and wept.

Oh, Grand-mamma, I thought, why didn't you tell me all this when you were alive? Suddenly I remembered my first night under that roof, and how I had been wakened from sleep by someone kissing me, very lightly.

Now I knew who it had been. Poor lady, so proud, so kind, and yet, Jonas Wilkins said she had been hard with her only son when he had dallied with one of the maids at Swalewell Keep.

We had given luncheon for the people who had attended the funeral, and some had stayed until after the will was read. The house was quiet now; I had afternoon tea in my room, and decided I would rest until dinner. I would see Alec then.

I longed to see him alone, and yet, I dreaded it. What would he think of me now — now that he knew I was Mrs. Dewbrey's grandchild?

Not only that, but a love child — a by-blow?

Penelope Campion's words came back tauntingly. So too did those of old Wilkins — ' 'Appen the old lady will see thee all right' — I lay on the bed, wrestling with my emotions until it was time to get ready for dinner.

I chose a black chiffon gown from my newly made mourning garments. It was simply cut, but very becoming, with a low neckline, and a basque which moulded my figure perfectly.

I would put a bold front on, however I felt.

'Put my hair in ringlets, Alice.'

'Yes, madam.'

I noticed she addressed me as madam now. I wondered what the other servants would think; no doubt they would be discussing me below stairs. With expert hands, Alice dressed my hair, and on a sudden impulse I took Hugh's gift to me out of the drawer, and fastened it round my neck. The effect of the black dress, my white skin, and the garnet and ruby necklace was exciting.

That night I would dine alone with Alec, and I wanted to look beautiful for him. Things did not work out as I had planned, though. Alec was missing from the dinner table. I waited as long as possible, then had dinner served, and ate it alone. I had little appetite; the loneliness of the room depressed me, and where was Alec?

Eventually I withdrew to Mrs. Dewbrey's sitting-room, and sat at the rosewood piano which I had so often played for her pleasure. As I slowly let my fingers wander over the keys I found myself drifting into playing the tune which Alec had once played as a duet with me.

The door opened, very quietly, and he stood there.

'Alec!' I exclaimed. 'Why, what is wrong?'

I had never seen him anything but immaculate; tonight, though, there was something curiously dishevelled about his appearance. He moved forward, and with a shock I realised what was wrong with him. He was drunk!

I stood up, hardly able to believe my eyes.

'No, don't stop playing. You look charming sitting there,' he said, his voice slightly slurred. He came up and stood behind me, his hands on my bare shoulders. During the months I had lived at Ditchford Hall I had never seem him have more than two glasses of wine with his dinner, indeed, sometimes he drank water. I knew that he drank brandy when entertaining other gentlemen, but always in moderation.

The idea that he would ever take too much alcohol under any circumstances had never occurred to me. I felt afraid.

'I waited and waited for you at dinner . . . ' I began.

'You are beautiful,' he said, ignoring my remark. 'Beautiful — tempting — everything to make a man want you.'

He seized me tightly in his arms, and covered my face and neck with kisses. I strained away, breathless, frightened.

This was not the Alec Dewbrey I knew, but a stranger, a man who appeared to have lost the respect he once showed me.

'Beautiful — alone in this great house — mistress of it,' he went on, his kisses fierce on my lips, his hands caressing me without restraint. He suddenly caught hold of the garnet necklace, his eyes narrowing.

'And where did you get this fine jewellery?'

'If you must know, Hugh Stacey gave me it when we became engaged,' I gasped. 'Now please — let me go!'

'So Stacey gave you it — a betrothal gift, no less. Yes, you were right about that, my dear, and I was wrong. I said Stacey had no intention of marrying you. My apologies — he had every intention!'

With a sudden movement I managed to wrench myself away. I felt sickened by his behaviour.

'You're drunk!' I said scornfully. 'I'll

leave you to sleep it off.' I fled from the room, fearful that he would prevent me. I hurried to my bedroom and once inside I locked the door, and stood panting behind it.

The day had begun with tension and worry; it had ended with bitter humiliation. I had not known how Alec would react to that will, but I had never dreamed he would make me feel as he had — a woman to be taken lightly — a woman who was merely — 'everything to make a man want you' . . .

I walked over to the bed, and began to unhook my gown, hoping that I would be able to manage without ringing for Alice.

Try as I could, I seemed unable to escape this web of unhappiness. I had thought Alec truly loved me — that his love would have been strong enough to stand this test. Now I saw the folly of trusting any man; all they wanted of a woman was that she serve their purpose, whatever it happened to be at the time.

* * *

The next morning I decided to breakfast in my bedroom. I doubted if Alec Dewbrey would appear for breakfast; anyway, if he did, I would not be there. I rose late, and Alice took some time helping me to dress. She was *my* maid now, I thought.

It crossed my mind that I would probably make some changes in the household staff, and yet, it was still difficult for me to fully realise that Ditchford Hall was mine.

I thought of Norfolk, and how that was where I wanted to be. I could not write about the will; I wanted to go home and tell my parents all about it. For although I now knew they were no relation to me, I still thought of them as being my parents. I wanted to hear their side of the story.

To my surprise, Alec Dewbrey appeared for luncheon. He looked paler than usual, but composed; as well turned out as ever.

'Good day, Miss Meredith,' he said.

So it was Miss Meredith again now. I sat looking down at my table napkin.

'Good day,' I said quietly. I was not going to say any more. If he had a mind to talk, I would listen.

He waited until the butler left the room.

'I must apologise for my behaviour last night. I realise how distressing it must have been for you. I assure you, you will have no further cause for complaint.'

'I am only too ready to forget the incident,' I said.

I thought in a detached way how excellent the luncheon was, and what little appetite I felt for it. Alec Dewbrey appeared to feel still less.

'I shall be moving my belongings out of Ditchford Hall as soon as possible,' he said.

'Moving . . . ' I began, and then composed myself.

'Yes. You are the mistress here, but I am not the master. I shall be moving to

Swalewell Keep.'

I was speechless with shock and surprise. Whatever I had imagined, I had never thought of Ditchford Hall without Alec Dewbrey.

'I find myself in an extremely embarrassing position, Miss Meredith. You must see, I could not stay here without arousing unpleasant gossip. I advise you to have some older lady living here after I have gone, in the capacity of adviser and chaperon. Perhaps you know of someone?'

'Thank you for your kindly concern,' I replied, not without an edge of sarcasm in my voice. 'Pray do not worry about my need for a chaperon. The need will cease to exist when you go.'

I was bitterly hurt by his behaviour, and I had the satisfaction of seeing his lips tighten when I said that.

'My real worry is the running of my estate,' I added, forcing myself to eat the chicken cutlets. I was determined to appear indifferent towards him. If he was taking this attitude, then I would press the sharp thorn into his flesh. I emphasised '*my estate*'.

'You will find Tulloch an excellent man in the running of your estate. I will leave things in good order for you.'

'I'm much obliged, sir.'

I could not trust myself to say any more. Although I had kept my voice steady, I knew that my face was flushed. How swiftly he had changed after the reading of the will, I thought. Only the day before the funeral he had held me in his arms and told me how he wanted to see me happy.

So much for murmured words of love; so much for Alec Dewbrey's affection. After some more remarks concerning the estate, he left the table, saying he had a number of matters to attend to. He was not alone in that. I went into Mrs. Dewbrey's sitting-room, and had to remind myself that it was now mine.

I penned a letter home, saying that I had a lot to tell them, and that I had been left 'a good deal' by Mrs. Dewbrey.

I added that as soon as her nephew left, I was coming home for a brief stay, to tell them all about it.

I decided the details could wait until I saw them. For the next few days I only met Alec Dewbrey occasionally; when I did, his manner was correct and formal. I knew that he was preparing to leave Ditchford Hall.

Try as I could, I was unable to understand his strange behaviour on the night of the funeral.

The way he had kissed me — had seized the necklace — and admitted that he had been wrong about Hugh Stacey's intentions. It mattered little now, anyway. I had been through so many emotions that I felt completely drained.

Too many disillusionments had come my way; it seemed to me I could trust no one, much less be foolish enough to feel affection for a man.

22

The train pulled up, and already I had glimpsed Papa, Mama, and Emma on the platform waiting for me. Mama looked thinner — and Emma had grown. My family, my dear, darling family, no matter who my rightful parents were.

I was waving from the carriage window — Papa was handing down my baggage, and I was hugging and kissing Mama and Emma and trying not to cry.

Although we talked throughout the journey back in the dogcart, I said little about Ditchford Hall. I slipped my arm through Mama's as we walked up the path to the vicarage.

I was glad that Georgina was spending a few weeks with an aunt in London; I had outgrown the exchanging of girlish confidences with her; too much had happened to me.

'Well, Debbie,' said Mama, as we entered the house, 'you're quite grown up, now.'

It was a strange feeling to be back in the shabby but comfortable vicarage. I could almost have thought that going away was part of a dream, and that all the strange and unbelievable things which had happened to me at Ditchford Hall were unreal. The rest of the household greeted me with obvious pleasure; nothing had changed, apparently.

I went over to the window in my bedroom, and saw the same tree outside. It was a blustery March day; I contrasted the view with the one from my window at Ditchford Hall.

'Everything looks so small,' I said, with a smile. My mother had followed me into the bedroom.

'And you look tired, Debbie,' she said quietly.

I turned away from the window, a lump suddenly coming into my throat. I wanted to appear cheerful; I was delighted at seeing them all again, and yet, I was bitterly unhappy.

'Mama . . . ' I began, and sank down onto the bed.

'Yes?'

'Mrs. Dewbrey has left me Ditchford Hall, and a great deal of property and money in her will.'

I heard Mama draw in her breath sharply.

'She was my grandmother, wasn't she?'

'Did she tell you so?'

'Not while she was alive. Only in her will was I named as being her son's daughter. Mama, I'm not your child, am I? I know who my mother was — she was Sarah Bailey, wasn't she?'

I fought to control my emotions; I could see that Mama was close to tears as well.

'Yes, she was. And she came to us because she had no one — she was an orphan, and the people who had befriended her turned her away. She was going to have a child.'

'Tell me about her,' I said, wiping my eyes.

'She was, well, very pretty, Debbie. And she was gay and high-spirited before everyone turned against her. I felt that if she had not been an orphan — if she had had careful guidance in her life, she would have behaved more prudently. We took her in, because we thought it was the right and Christian thing to do. We became fond of her, and we did not admire Mrs. Caldecott at the Hall for ignoring the poor girl's existence.'

She was silent for a moment, as though looking into the past.

'Sarah was very proud. She was different from the other girls in service round about. And of course, she had suitors by the dozen — she could have had her pick of the village boys, but she would have nothing to do with them. Small wonder, really, when she had attracted the Caldecotts' son.'

'And where was my father?'

'He was in America. They were so

young, Debbie. Will Caldecott had led a very sheltered life — he seemed not to know how to deal with responsibilities at all. And Sarah, although I think she was basically more practical, fell in with his plans. He wanted to make a life in the New World, and then came the news from Ditchford Hall that he had died of a fever. The poor girl loved him — she was distraught with grief. Your father and I tried to comfort her, but she seemed beyond comfort. Will Caldecott's mother knew that Sarah was living with us, and that she was about to have her son's child.'

'What did she do?'

'Nothing. She sat up there in that great house, cold, proud, and unforgiving. And Sarah sat in our house, equally proud.'

'And what happened then?'

'You were born; a frail, seven months baby, and poor Sarah slipped out of the world a few hours later. She begged us to keep you, to christen you Deborah, and to bring you up, she said, prudently and strictly, as if you were our child. We promised to do this. Papa had already got a living here, and we knew we would be moving. However, we deemed it only right to let Mrs. Caldecott know that we were going to keep you, and bring you up in our name.'

She paused again before continuing.

'Your papa went to Ditchford Hall to see Mrs. Caldecott, as she was then. She received him, but not very cordially. He told her that Sarah had asked us to keep her baby, and asked if she wished to help in any way. She said no. He then told her where we would be living, and said that as she was your grandmother we would let her know how you were progressing, if she was interested. She said she was not, but many years later, just before you were eighteen, she did write, Debbie, and ask if you could go as her companion. Well, Papa had promised all those years ago — and you know he would not go back on his word.'

'I know.'

I sat on the bed with Mama, and thought how mixed their feelings must have been, when out of the blue, a mellowed and repentant old lady had asked for her grandchild.

'She knew, of course, that we had brought you up as our own,' went on Mama. 'Sometimes I didn't know if it was right to let you think you were ours, but we promised Sarah on her deathbed.'

'Yes, it was right,' I said slowly. 'Except that now, even though I have wealth and possessions, I am but a love child. And there will always be tongues to whisper that Will Caldecott was not my father.'

I thought of Penelope Campion.

'There was one thing which your papa didn't tell your grandmother, though. It was Sarah's idea not to, she was so bitter at Will's mother's attitude. They ran off together, and then he got this notion about America.

'In her condition she could not travel at the time, so he left her in England.

They had little money, for his mother had cut him off — and other money he was to inherit was tied up until he was twenty-five I believe — I don't know the details. Anyway, he dreamed, as many young men do, of making a fortune in America. So he sailed abroad, with never a doubt in his mind that the Wilkins would give her a home for the time being. But they would have nothing to do with the poor girl — I believe they let her spend one night there, and then turned her out. She was so broken-hearted that only Papa and I knew the whole truth about the matter.'

'The whole truth?'

'Yes. They *were* married, Debbie. They planned that she should join him after you were born, and make a new life together abroad. He truly loved her, I believe, and she did him. Letters took a long time, though. He gave her an address to write to in New York. She wrote several letters, but before she heard from him came the news of his death. It was terrible.'

'They *were* married,' I repeated. 'Are you sure? Do you think she just pretended that?'

'We thought so when she first told us, but the people who owned this house in New York returned Sarah's letters, and your father's private papers. He died in hospital there — I believe he was ill when the boat actually docked, and became progressively worse. From what I could make out, the news of his death went to Mrs. Caldecott at Ditchford Hall. This was understandable, because if Sarah's letters to him had not arrived at that time, he probably gave his next-of-kin as Mrs. Caldecott, Swalewell village. It was a tragic error; instead of the news going to his young wife, it went to his mother.

'We buried Sarah in Swalewell churchyard, under her maiden name of Bailey. Then, a few days before we left the house for good, a package came addressed to Mrs. Sarah Caldecott.

It was a kind note for her from an

American lady, saying how Will Caldecott had stayed at their house, and how they had at first attempted to nurse him themselves. She enclosed Sarah's letters to Will, a letter written by him to her, but never posted — a few other items, and their marriage certificate. I have kept these things, Debbie, in case it was ever necessary to prove your parentage. You see, *we* knew you were a Caldecott, and born in wedlock, but your grandmother never knew it.'

I sat, trying to take this in.

'But she left me so much,' I said. 'She left me all that, thinking that I was a love child.'

'Then it shows that she forgave everything, and tried to make amends towards her son. She knew that it was wrong to let the Caldecott inheritance go to someone not of Caldecott blood. Not only that, but she must have loved you for yourself.'

'I believe she was fond of me,' I said. 'Mama, she was not a cold-hearted person such as you have described. She was kind and good — the night before she became very ill, she held me close, and kissed me, as though she knew the end was near.'

'That may be so, Debbie, but at the time she behaved harshly towards her son and Sarah. She loved him, and she was proud of him. He ran off with a parlour maid, and the whole Riding buzzed with the scandal. She must have regretted it over the years, and she made amends in the end.'

A great relief flooded through me. I was not a by-blow — a love child! I was a true Caldecott, born in wedlock, and nothing could take that away. I thought of Penelope Campion again. She was of no account . . . but Alec! He had gone out of my life; indeed, I had heard that having moved into Swalewell Keep, he had departed for London almost immediately.

I turned to Mama and embraced her.

'You and Papa will always be my parents,' I said. 'And Emma and Albert and John are my brothers and sister.'

Mama was very moved, and so was I. I could not condemn them for not telling my grandmother I was born in wedlock; they had carried out my mother's wishes to the end.

And something of Sarah's cold pride stirred in me; I could prove my parentage if I wished, but I wanted to be accepted for myself.

I planned to stay at the vicarage for two weeks, and then return to Ditchford Hall, and have the place prepared for my family to come and stay for a while. I knew there were many matters to attend to; there was some talk of Cousin Maud living with me at Ditchford Hall, and I smiled sadly to myself.

Mama was as anxious about my welfare as ever, and like Alec Dewbrey, she felt I had the need of a chaperon.

Concerning him, I did not confide in her. I felt I could discuss him with no one. Papa and Mama were unanimous in agreeing that my place was at Ditchford Hall. I vowed to myself that I would help them in every way possible; even then I could never repay them, I knew, for the years of selfless devotion which they had given me.

* * *

I was back in Ditchford Hall, with the tender greenness of April unfolding around me. I was nineteen now; it was a twelvemonth since I had first come there as a young lady of 'some eighteen summers'.

Every morning I went to the stables and had Pansy saddled, and then rode in the grounds for an hour. Misty was a long-legged yearling now; he would nuzzle me with his velvety nose, and gaze at me with his mournful, dreamy eyes. I had told Emma about him, and she was eager to see him. My main pleasure came from planning to make my family happy when they came.

I felt I had a duty, too, to my dead mother. I had her grave located in Swalewell churchyard. It was just a patch of overgrown weeds, but I arranged for it to be dug and tended, and ordered a headstone, bearing the name Sarah Caldecott.

It was just about a year since Alec Dewbrey had shown me round the church, and we had gazed at the wild, desolate moorland together. I remembered what he had said about the spring coming, and the creatures who had survived the winter running and playing in the sunshine.

Well, I had survived the winter, unlike my grandmother, or poor Hugh Stacey. But as for running and playing in the sunshine — no. I was like an animal who had survived, but who crawled around, deeply wounded.

As I rode back on Pansy, I thought about the past year, and how foolish and trusting I had been. I thought of the evening I had spent at the Campions, when Ram Singh had been asked to tell my fortune.

' . . . I must warn the memsahib against people who would work evil

. . . the memsahib is looking for happiness — it will not come in the way she thinks . . . there will be great sadness first . . . '

Great sadness. How very true those words had been.

A great sadness seemed to hang over Ditchford Hall; seemed to linger in the walled garden, and the stables.

The slender figure of Mrs. Dewbrey would be seen no more, and the whole house mourned her passing.

But more than that, 'Mr. Alec' no longer strode the grounds with Horatio at his heel, or talked to John Stubbs in the stable yard.

Only I remained; the last of the Caldecotts, mistress of Ditchford Hall; the rightful heiress.

And with all that, a lonely unhappy girl.

23

It was a chill spring afternoon, and I was talking to Tresset. I had not felt well for the past two or three days, although I could not really say what ailed me.

I decided to have a walk in the grounds, thinking I would feel brighter for it. Overhead, heavy rainclouds threatened; the recent fine weather seemed about to break. Tresset remarked on this as I left him; in fact he cautioned me against going too far from the house.

I walked round the potting sheds, and the next moment I was transfixed with amazement. There was a yelping bark, and Horatio flung himself at me, his tail wagging with undisguised delight.

'Horatio!' I cried. 'Horatio!'

I bent to pat him. He was dripping

wet, and I glanced around, half thinking Alec would not be far away, but there was no one about. How then had Horatio suddenly appeared? I patted his head and quietened him as best I could. He must have swum across Swalewell Beck, that was the only explanation. No doubt he had fretted over at Swalewell Keep, with his master away in London. After all, Ditchford Hall was home to him — he had lived there all his life; how could he be happy anywhere else?

I stroked his wet head. He would have to be taken back, of course. But how? I could send him back with one of the servants, but I decided against it. Next to Alec Dewbrey, Horatio loved me, and I wanted to take him back myself. It would have to be that afternoon, too, or he would be missed, and they would be searching frantically for him.

Apart from that, I was afraid that if I let him stay overnight, parting with him would be too hard.

'Come, Horatio,' I said softly. I began

to walk in the direction of the river, and the trusting creature walked beside me, stopping to shake his fur from time to time.

The boathouse was just the same; the boat was just the same; there was no sign of Tulloch and Keeper. I had never been near the river since that terrible night when Alec had rowed out after me. I thought of the boat which we had left to drift; I had never mentioned it to him. I supposed it had gone through the weir, and been lost.

I unmoored the remaining boat. 'Come on, Horatio.'

He jumped in the boat, and I began to row. It was a strange, nostalgic feeling to be rowing once more down that river, with its many associations. A year ago I had persuaded Dan Tulloch to let me take a boat out alone, and so many things had happened to me because of that.

Once in the boat, I had an inexplicable desire to take it down to the place where Hugh and I used to meet in the afternoons.

Horatio sat quietly while I rowed, and then the first drops of rain began to fall. Tresset had said it would rain within the half hour; he was usually right about the weather.

I was wearing my cloak with a hood, so I was not unduly worried; nevertheless, as it came on more heavily, I decided I would have to pull into the bank and take shelter. It was no use trying to reach the place where I used to meet Hugh; the rain was driving so heavily I could scarcely see.

There was a clump of bushes jutting out over the bank, and I began to steer the boat alongside. By this time my cloak was streaming with water, and Horatio began to give worried little barks. I brought the boat in, and stepped onto the bank, wetting my feet thoroughly in the process.

'Come on, Horatio,' I said, but to my annoyance he sat barking, still in the boat. Desperately I seized his collar, but he snarled, refusing to move. In the confusion I lost the mooring rope; the boat moved out of my reach, and began to drift downstream.

'Horatio!' I cried, in terror. 'Horatio!'

He was a yard away from me, he was two yards, three yards, then, when he realised he was in a moving boat by himself, with a loud yelp he sprang over the side and swam towards me.

A few moments later he was safe on the bank with me, while the boat went on drifting downstream, destined for the weir.

I shuddered. I was stranded now, on the Swalewell Keep side of the river, in one of the heaviest downpours of rain I had experienced while living at Ditchford Hall.

The tree we were standing under provided inadequate shelter. We huddled together; Horatio trembled, shook his fur, and trembled again, whimpering with sheer misery.

I looked across at Swalewell Keep, rain-misted and mysterious. Would it be better to make a dash for it, take shelter in the woods half way, and then go on to the house with Horatio? It had seemed such a simple matter to row the dog across the river, but it hadn't turned out that way at all. I would have to wait at Swalewell Keep, and take a carriage back to Ditchford Hall.

The only other way was the long walk which took me near Jonas Wilkins' cottage and the bridge; quite unthinkable in such heavy rain.

I began to run through the blinding wetness towards the woods, with Horatio at my heels, barking. We had almost reached the sheltering trees when there was a burning pain in my left ankle, and with a scream I found myself lying full length on the sodden earth, crying with pain.

Horatio stood barking, expecting me to get up and run again. I felt physically sick with shock. The ground was rough, and I had sprained my ankle badly, I could tell that. My cloak clung to me like a soaking blanket, my hood had come down, and rain beat on my hair and face.

Shaken and sick, I pulled myself up into a sitting position. Horatio knew that something was wrong. He tried to lick my face, then crouched beside me, whining again. The pain in my ankle was unbearable; already it was swelling rapidly.

To get shelter I would have to crawl along as best I could. I began to do this, slowly and painfully, in the direction of the woods. Before long my skirt was torn, and my knees sore.

I was obliged to keep stopping to rest. Horatio walked slowly along, too, whining softly. He would not leave me, but I sensed his unease. He barked every time I stopped.

The woods seemed to be no nearer, and I was worried by a growing feeling of weakness. Pain stabbed me continually; I had gingerly removed my shoe, and was appalled to see my ankle and instep already enormously swollen. I wondered miserably if I had broken a bone. To make matters worse, I had left my watch in the house, and had no means of knowing the time.

After what seemed hours, I dragged myself into the fringe of the woods, and lay down exhausted on the damp earth.

It was still too early in the year for the leaves to be thick enough overhead to afford complete shelter from such a deluge. Even so, it was better than the open country.

Horatio and I lay there, oozing water and shivering. I felt too weak and spent to move again. The rain did not cease, and I could feel a sort of numbness creeping over me.

The pain in my ankle was a relentless throb now, spreading right down my foot. The dog lay whimpering beside me. After a long time I raised my head and looked across at the old Keep.

It seemed miles away.

My head, shoulders and arms were all aching now. I bitterly regretted the impulse which had made me take the boat out to bring Horatio back to Swalewell Keep. I lay there ill and exhausted, while the afternoon turned into a cold, wet, April evening. Horatio huddled his great bulk up against me; I felt his slobbering tongue lick my face. It was growing darker, colder, mistier. At the slightest movement, the throbbing pain in my ankle turned to hot, searing agony.

* * *

A long, terrible darkness was all around me . . . there was pain everywhere, every bone ached, and my throat was parched and sore. A great, warm weight seemed to be pressing down on me — surely I was dreaming? With jumping starts I woke and slept, and woke again, moaning. Then, suddenly, the darkness had gone; only the pain remained.

The great warm weight had gone, too; my teeth chattered, my body trembled and shivered with cold. After a while, I seemed to be floating away from my body, away from cold and misery . . .

I could hear a loud, persistent noise; something in my dulled senses registered that it was a dog barking. Then there was the sound of voices shouting — everything was confused and unreal.

But somebody was holding me — that seemed real enough — and a face seemed to float in front of me, and fade away. I heard a voice calling: 'Debbie! Debbie!' over and over again.

I opened my eyes. They seemed to have lead weights on them. Why, it was Alec Dewbrey's face! How frightened he looked. I slipped back into the darkness again.

For a long time it was darkness, and murmuring voices, and faces that came and went. Alec Dewbrey's face; Dr. Denton's face — then Alice's face. Perhaps it was all a nightmare, because I seemed to wake up properly from a long, unpleasant dream.

I was in bed, in a big, strange room.

'Where am I?' I asked.

Alice appeared, smiling. 'You're at Swalewell Keep, ma'am. Mr. Dewbrey had me brought here to help look after you.'

'Swalewell Keep! Have I been ill?'

'Yes, indeed, ma'am — but Dr. Denton said if you woke up you must not talk much. He will be here to see you soon.'

I drifted off to sleep again, but this time it was pleasantly dreamless. When I woke, Dr. Denton and Alec Dewbrey were both in the room. I was in a richly curtained four-poster bed in a vast and very beautifully furnished bedroom.

'How are you feeling now, Miss Meredith?' enquired Dr. Denton, smiling encouragingly. 'You've had us worried these past few days. You'll have to tell us all about it.'

My eyes met Alec's, and to my chagrin, I began to cry.

'She's still very weak,' I heard the doctor say.

'My ankle hurts,' I sobbed.

'It's a nasty sprain — and you've been ill besides.'

'I'll give her something to make her

sleep. She needs another poultice on, too,' said Dr. Denton.

The next day I felt very much better. I learnt that I'd had congestion of the lungs, and had been very ill for over a week. The crisis had passed, though, and I was definitely improving. I lay in bed, propped up on lace-trimmed pillows, while Alice gently coaxed my hair into some sort of order, and helped me with my toilet.

I looked at myself in a hand mirror; I was thinner, and very pale, with eyes that looked too big for my face. Alice chattered away eagerly.

'We searched the place for you — in all that rain, madam,' she said. 'The last person who talked to you was Tresset — we were that worried! Then Dan Tulloch found the boat gone! Well, that really scared the life out of us — we told the police — the boat was found the next day — it had gone through the weir.'

'Oh, dear,' I said. 'I've worried a lot of people, and I never intended to. All that happened was that Mr. Dewbrey's dog had swum across from this side of the river, and I thought I would row him back. Then it began to rain heavily, and when I brought the boat in to the bank, Horatio wouldn't get out of it, and I lost the mooring rope.

'He finally jumped out when it started to drift away, and there we were in the pouring rain. And, of course, I was stranded, Alice. We ran to the woods for shelter, and I fell and sprained my ankle. It was terrible, because I had to crawl to the woods, and I was too ill and exhausted to go further, once I got there. I think this illness was coming on in any case . . . Horatio stayed with me — where is he now? Where is Horatio?'

'He's safe, ma'am. Mr. Dewbrey wouldn't let him in the room when you were so poorly. He had only just come back from London the day before, and he was in Halifield on business. I heard him telling the doctor how Horatio had barked and barked, and led him to the place where you were lying in the woods. Horatio had been missing, too, but it was night when Mr. Dewbrey came back from Halifield, and I suppose there was nothing they could do until morning.'

She paused, to concentrate on combing out a tangle in my hair.

'Well, it seems in the morning Horatio turned up, and led them to you. But John Stubbs was round at Swalewell Keep first thing in the morning to see if you were there — Mr. Dewbrey was nearly frantic, ma'am; the boat gone over the weir — and Horatio missing as well . . . '

She broke off, as if she had said too much.

Out of the blurred memory of that morning, I remembered the fear on Alec Dewbrey's face.

Alice dabbed my brow with cologne. Then she tidied up the toilet things, and left the room. I lay thinking.

My mind went back over the twelvemonth I had known Alec Dewbrey.

Everything he did seemed to stem from a firm sense of duty. His obligations were always carried out scrupulously. I had tried to dismiss him from my mind after he had left Ditchford Hall. I told myself that he had only been amusing himself with me, and had taken the quickest way out of an awkward situation when he had found that instead of being a mere paid companion, I was part of the Caldecotts' scandalous past, and one of the wealthiest women in the Riding.

Was that the truth, though? The weak tears pricked my eyes again, for I still loved him. And now I was under his roof, and he had brought my maid over from Ditchford Hall to help care for me. Later in the day he came to see me, and brought Horatio, who propped his front paws on the bed, and wagged his tail with delight. Alec enquired gravely how I was feeling.

'Very much better, thank you. I am sorry I have inconvenienced you like this.'

'It is hardly an inconvenience — I am thankful you were found when you were. After the way you nursed me last winter, I am glad to be of any service. I am still at a loss, though, to understand how Horatio came to be with you, and how the rowing boat drifted away down the river.'

Briefly I told him the story, as I had recounted it to Alice.

'I can only think Horatio went looking for me,' he said slowly. 'I had been away in London, and no doubt he had been fretting for me. Then, as soon as I got back to Swalewell Keep, I was obliged to go into Halifield on business. He must have thought he would find me at Ditchford Hall.'

We were both silent for some time.

'Do you like Swalewell Keep?' I asked finally.

'In its way it has an ancient beauty, I suppose. Succeeding generations of Staceys have rebuilt it in parts, altered it, tried to modernise it, and generally improve it — sometimes with little success. Whatever has been done, though, the basic character of the place remains unchanged — one is always conscious of living in an old Norman fortress.'

'I am glad you are content here,' I said.

'I did not say that I was content. But if you are talking about contentment, I hope all is well with you at Ditchford Hall.'

'The days pass . . . '

I turned my face away, as I knew my eyes were filling with tears.

'And have you friends — a companion? Have you a lady to live with you yet?'

'I did not know my welfare was so important to you.'

I could not help that bitter remark from slipping out.

'Debbie, I told you once that I wanted your happiness more than anything . . . '

'And then everything changed, didn't it, after the will was read?'

'How could it be otherwise, under the circumstances?'

'It could not have been otherwise, I suppose. I was named as Mrs. Dewbrey's grandchild — the natural daughter of her son.'

'Debbie, it was not *that* which made me change my ideas! Aunt Caroline had talked to me, and said she hoped I would behave fittingly towards you after her death. Then, when the will was read, I learnt you were no longer a companion, but an heiress. The thought that people would say I had married you for that reason was uppermost in my mind. I knew how few men you had met — I felt it would be taking advantage of your youth and inexperience. Why, you have never even had a season in London . . . '

He broke off, and I saw how very moved he was.

'Debbie, I can't bear the idea of you having a season in London!'

This was the vulnerable side of him, which I had glimpsed before.

'After the will was read I had to wrestle with myself — with my natural feelings, and what I thought was my duty. That night I felt I could not face you — I drank too much — and then, when I did see you, you were so beautiful! You were wearing a necklace which Hugh Stacey had given you — I was mad with jealousy, thinking how he had wanted you — and how other men would want you! I thought it best to get out of Ditchford Hall as soon as possible.'

'And my feelings,' I said. 'Did you think what *my* feelings must have been — you talked of love, and then rejected me when I needed you most? As it happens, I found out before Mrs. Dewbrey died that I was her granddaughter. Old Jonas Wilkins told me — my mother lived with the Wilkins in their cottage. Her name was Sarah Bailey; she was a parlour maid here, and my father fell in love with her,' I said proudly.

'Then some of the local people must

have known about it. I had no idea . . . my aunt was very fond of you, and treated you more like a daughter than a companion, I know. But she never confided in me that you were her grand-daughter — how did you first suspect it?'

'Miss Campion called at the house, and told me I was a by-blow of the Caldecotts,' I said bluntly. 'Or, rather, she said I was a by-blow, and that Mrs. Dewbrey *thought* her son was my father. Anyway, the following day I went to see Wilkins, because he shouted 'Caldecott' when he first saw me, and the day you were shot he said I was a Caldecott.'

'Miss Campion came to Ditchford Hall, and called you a by-blow,' repeated Alec angrily. 'How dare she!'

'She did not feel kindly towards me,' I said. 'I have no doubt you will know why.'

'Miss Campion will soon be announcing her engagement, I believe. A certain Mr. Roger Barnstaple is eager to make her his wife. After my aunt died, there was much speculation in the district concerning my next move. I must have disappointed a number of people.'

'Miss Campion is saving her face,' I said.

'Her behaviour towards you was unforgivable — I had no idea she had come to the house insulting you . . . '

'It is of no consequence now.'

'Did she say I would soon lose interest in you if I knew you were a — er — love child?'

'Words to that effect,' I said, remembering her vile insults.

'Debbie, I loved you for yourself alone — I always will do — but when you suddenly had great wealth and possessions — well, it was something which I had never imagined happening. I thought Aunt Caroline may well have left you some small legacy . . . '

He paused, and I remembered Dryden's words that winter day when he had come to see me:

'Mr. Dewbrey is a very fine gentleman . . . from my experience of him, he is above a great many things.'

'But surely, you are not poor yourself,' I said hesitantly.

'Not exactly.'

There was a long, thoughtful silence.

'I want to take care of you, Debbie,' said Alec, breaking it. 'My life has been meaningless without you. I had to come back north, even though it was to live at Swalewell Keep. And then, when John Stubbs came that morning to ask if you were here by any chance — when he said you were missing — and they were talking of dragging the river!'

I saw the remembered shock and horror on his face.

'I've been away, too,' I said quietly. 'I went back to the vicarage — and learnt the truth about my parents — and how I came to be brought up by the Merediths. And, by the way, I am not a love child. My parents were married, and my rightful name is Caldecott. My grandmother never knew that, though.

My mother died a few hours after I was born.'

He reached out, and clasped my hands in his.

'If she was like you, Debbie, sweet and lovely, and brave, perhaps your father thought he had found something finer and better than the fashionable beauties parading around him.'

'They paid dearly for loving each other, anyway,' I said with a sigh.

'When two people fall in love, I suppose they don't always think where it will lead them,' said Alec thoughtfully. 'And old families, well, they can never escape from their past, somehow. It's the same with old houses. This place is mine now, and yet, there are times when it seems to be full of the Staceys and their dreams.'

'I don't think Horatio likes living at Swalewell Keep,' I said. 'I have a feeling that before long he will be crossing the river again.'

'I have a feeling . . . ' Alec broke off, and strode over to the window. Outside was the bright sunshine of a spring day.

'Debbie,' he said. 'Do you think Aunt Caroline thought that I might be behaving fittingly towards you by marrying you? Do you?'

He turned and came towards me, and Horatio, stirred by the excitement in his master's voice, jumped up onto the bed beside me, wagging his tail.

'You could not behave any more fittingly towards me,' I said, hardly able to speak for emotion. 'Let me be the judge of that, Alec.'

The next moment his arms were around me, and our lips met in a long kiss that blotted out the past, and gave tender assurance of happiness to come.

'And where do you want to live — here — or at Ditchford Hall?' asked Alec, some time later.

It seemed incredible that I could be mistress of either of these beautiful places, or both, if I chose.

'Caldecotts should stay on the other side of the river,' I said. 'Old Jonas Wilkins told me that — he said one of the Staceys had put a curse on any Caldecott that crossed the river on to the Stacey land — or what should be Stacey land. Yes, you may smile, Alec, but judging by my experiences up to now, it's a risk I prefer not to take. Lease Swalewell Keep, or sell it — do what you will with it, but please let us live at Ditchford Hall when we are married.'

'I knew you would say that. I only gave you the choice as a matter of formality.' He laughed.

I patted Horatio.

'You're coming back to Ditchford Hall,' I told him, and happiness went through my whole being, even though I was still tired and weak.

I would be going back to Ditchford Hall soon, to live there among the dreams and memories of my ancestors; to put down my roots with Alec Dewbrey.

Perhaps some day, when I was old, I would take out my diary, and relive the past. I would tell my children, and my children's children, the story of that strange and wonderful year I had spent at Ditchford Hall, when I was a young lady of some eighteen summers.

THE END